Changeling Press, LLC

ChangelingPress.com

Iron/Blades Duet
A Dixie Reapers Bad Boys Romance
Harley Wylde

Iron/Blades Duet
A Dixie Reapers Bad Boys Romance
Harley Wylde

All rights reserved.
Copyright ©2024 Harley Wylde

ISBN: 978-1-60521-925-7

Publisher:
Changeling Press LLC
315 N. Centre St.
Martinsburg, WV 25404
ChangelingPress.com

Printed in the U.S.A.

Editor: Crystal Esau
Cover Artist: Bryan Keller

The individual stories in this anthology have been previously released in E-Book format.

No part of this publication may be reproduced or shared by any electronic or mechanical means, including but not limited to reprinting, photocopying, or digital reproduction, without prior written permission from Changeling Press LLC.

This book contains sexually explicit scenes and adult language which some may find offensive and which is not appropriate for a young audience. Changeling Press books are for sale to adults, only, as defined by the laws of the country in which you made your purchase.

Table of Contents

Iron (Hades Abyss MC 11)
A Dixie Reapers Bad Boys Romance
Harley Wylde

Nari -- Pain. Humiliation. Those are the things my father taught me, and every man I've met since has done the same. Running away from home didn't fix anything. Now I'm nineteen and back in the town my family calls home. I haven't told them I'm here, and I don't plan to. But I also didn't count on a biker giving me a ride and leaving me at the Hades Abyss compound. They say they'll help me, but can I trust them? What if they're just as bad as all the others?

Iron -- I'm no stranger to the darker side of life. Sometimes I'm the monster lurking in the shadows. Still, there's a line I won't cross. I will never harm an innocent woman or child. The moment I saw the tiny Asian woman cowering in front of Titan, I wanted to protect her from the world. She's been beaten, yet she's not broken. I've never met anyone like Nari before. Despite how timid she appears, she's stronger than she realizes. I know I'll do whatever it takes to make her smile and keep her safe, even if it means getting blood on my hands. The moment her family tries to take her from me, I'll show them what it means for Nari to be mine.

Prologue

Nari -- Three Years Ago

I could hear my stepsister screaming in the other room. One of her many tantrums. She was only one year younger than me, and yet she acted incredibly immature for her age. Even worse, my family let her. Although, could I really consider them my family anymore? At what point did you merely become strangers living in the same house?

Not for the first time I considered leaving this place. I wondered how long it would take them to realize I was gone. Then again, they would probably throw a celebration. The Kwon family would finally be rid of me. My father would have abandoned me long ago if it wouldn't have brought dishonor to the Kwon family. As long as I remained here, he could claim I was a bad daughter and lead people to believe he allowed me to stay due to his benevolent nature. There were times I wanted to expose all three of them as the horrible people they were.

It had been twelve years since my father remarried and moved us from Korea to the US. Thanks to Joon and my stepmother wanting to only speak English, I remembered very little Korean. They'd not only stolen my father and my home, but also my heritage.

What made Joon so special? Why did everyone always adore her and hate me? No one could see her for the spoiled, selfish girl I knew her to be.

Joon screamed some more, and I heard something shatter. The fact her crush had shown me the slightest bit of attention had made her completely lose it. It didn't matter that I didn't like the guy, or that he'd only been speaking to me in order to be polite. All the spoiled little bitch cared about was the fact he hadn't been paying her attention.

Everything went quiet, and I had a feeling it meant bad news for me. I could only imagine what Father had promised her in order to make Joon shut up. It could mean anything from confinement to complete and utter agony. Considering how much she hated me, something told me I was in for a beating. We'd been through this enough times for me to know my father would call the school and tell them I was sick, then I'd stay home until the marks faded. No matter how much I tried to brace myself, feeling the impact of the cane again and again always broke me. It wasn't only the pain, but also the fact my own father could do such a thing to me, and all because he preferred my stepsister.

No matter how many times I'd asked what I'd done wrong, he'd never responded. As I'd gotten older, I'd often wondered if I reminded him too much of my mother. From what I could remember he'd absolutely adored her. I'd been too small to recall anything about her death, and no one would tell me anyway. The way my father would glare at me made me wonder if I'd somehow been at fault.

I heard his footsteps and the thump of the cane as he came down the hall. Curling myself into a ball in the corner, I wondered if it wouldn't be better if he just killed me. How much longer could I survive something like this? The one time I'd tried to tell someone at school, my father and stepmother convinced them I was only seeking attention. There was no one on my side.

The door opened and I buried my face against my knees and covered my head with my arms. It wouldn't stop him from beating me, but I worried what would happen if I passed out. Ending things on my own terms was different from letting him kill me. There had been a time I thought my father would never do such a thing. Now I wondered -- if Joon asked him to take my life, would he even hesitate?

"You've brought this on yourself," he said. I didn't even get a chance to respond before the cane slammed into my arms. He didn't stop. Blow after blow landed on my legs, ribs, arms... and after I collapsed onto my stomach, he continued to hit me from my shoulders all the way to the soles of my feet.

By the time he finished, I could hear his labored breaths. I didn't dare look up. My father left the room without a word, and I heard him insert the key into the lock and twist it. I managed to crawl my way into the bathroom before I threw up. The pain left me dizzy, and tears streaked my cheeks.

I knew if I remained still, it would only be worse tomorrow. I filled the tub with cold water and managed to undress and pull myself into it. My teeth chattered and I gripped the sides of the tub to keep from sinking under the water. No matter how many times I'd thought death might be preferable, I refused to give them the satisfaction of knowing they'd driven me to take my own life. If I were going to end it all, it wouldn't be here at the house or right after a beating. I'd make sure they wouldn't be able to cover it up, and I would leave a note telling the world what kind of monsters they were.

Closing my eyes, I sent up a silent prayer that I could hold out a little longer. I either needed to find the courage to take my life -- or run away. The nightmare needed to end. Whatever it took, I had to escape from these people.

Chapter One

Nari

My cheek pressed into the carpet as Gio held me down. I knew I'd be covered in bruises within the hour, if I wasn't already. Nothing new. It seemed all I had to do was breathe in order to piss him off. I'd only stayed due to a lack of options. Leaving Gio would only mean taking a chance on someone else. Men didn't help runaway teens for nothing. They either made us drug mules, thieves, or prostitutes. I couldn't think of a way to escape. Everyone I'd ever trusted had betrayed me. Why should that change?

If things had been different, if my family had cared even a little, I never would have run away. Living at home had been awful, but my life on the streets was far worse.

"You stupid, worthless cunt! Where's my money?" he asked for the fifth time. As if my answer was suddenly going to change.

"I told you I don't have it. I couldn't find any work today, Gio." Or more accurately, I hadn't found a mark. Stealing was my forte.

He leaned in closer. "Then you have a choice, Nari. You can pay the money by spending a few nights at the house on Spruce, or you find a high-paying job before morning. Which is it going to be?"

I swallowed hard. It wasn't really a choice at all. I refused to go near drugs, and I really didn't want to be a whore. I couldn't understand the girls and women who chose that path. I didn't look down on them for it, but it wasn't something I'd ever voluntarily do. Of course, if I wanted a legal job, there was always the strip club. Except I hadn't really been blessed in the curves department. I didn't even need a bra. Who the hell would pay to watch me take my clothes off? Now, letting him use me as a whore in his brothel? That was a different story. Those men didn't much care what a woman looked like, and I knew he wouldn't be sending his top customers my way. All they wanted was a living woman to fuck, although it wouldn't surprise me if some didn't even care if I was alive when they fucked me. I'd learned the hard way just how screwed up people could be.

"I'll find a job," I said. "Please, Gio. I really tried."

He finally released me and stood. "Fine. By sunrise, you better have something lined up. If not, don't bother coming home. You either take your ass over to Spruce, or you better run."

As if running would do me any good. He'd track me down and things would be even worse. But I had to try. I refused to go down without a fight, or at the very least a last-ditch effort. If only I'd known I was heading in this direction the moment I walked out of my dad's house. Not once had I seen my picture on the news or in any papers. He'd never bothered to search for me. Why would he, when he had his precious Joon?

Maybe I could go home. Or at least back to my hometown. I didn't think Gio would ever think to look for me there. He knew how much I hated that place, and the hell I'd been through while I lived at home. Yeah. I should go back. I didn't bring in enough money for him to chase me across state lines.

I waited until Gio left, then packed a small backpack. It wasn't like I owned much anyway. Grabbing the little bit of cash I'd managed to hide, I shoved it into my satchel and left the house for the last time. One way or another, I was leaving this place behind. I didn't care if I had to hitchhike all the way back to Mississippi.

Every step made pain explode through my body. I stopped to put on my hoodie and made sure my face was mostly covered. I didn't need anyone seeing the marks on my body and stopping to ask questions. A rumble of a motorcycle came up behind me and slowed. I quickly glanced toward the street and realized the man was eyeing me.

I assessed his overall size and wondered if I could outrun him. Men prowling the streets for women always spelled trouble.

"Do you need a ride somewhere?" he asked.

I took in every detail of his appearance, from his Native American genes to the leather cut declaring him part of the Reckless Kings MC. I hadn't heard of them, but there was a group of bikers in my hometown -- Hades Abyss MC. They'd been a little scary, but I'd never heard of them hurting kids or anything. Was his club the same? Just because he looked rough and little scary didn't mean he was a bad guy. Sometimes, the ones who looked like wholesome decent men were the most vicious.

He sighed and inched the bike closer. "Look. My name is Crow. I'm not going to hurt you, but it looks like you're in some trouble and trying to get out of here. So you can get on the back of my bike and I'll take you as far as I can. Or you can keep walking and hope whoever you're running from doesn't catch up. With the way you're moving, I'm going to assume someone beat the hell out of you."

I winced. He'd noticed that? "I'm going to Mississippi."

"What part?" he asked.

"Ever heard of a club called the Hades Abyss? I'm going to that town," I said.

He nodded. "I know them. Get on and I'll make sure you get home. It's a little out of my way, but it's fine."

Without another thought, I climbed on behind him and put my arms around his waist. It wasn't my first time on a motorcycle, even if it had been years ago. It also wasn't the first time I'd put my trust in a stranger. He'd either keep me safe, or I'd trade one abusive asshole for another.

"I'm Nari," I said. "Thanks for the ride."

"Sure thing, kid. Hold on tight." He twisted the throttle, revving the engine, then eased the bike forward. As he picked up speed and shifted gears, the wind whipped the hood off my head. I closed my eyes and pressed my forehead to his back. For the first time in forever, I felt free.

I didn't know if I'd made the right choice, but there was no going back now. I knew my family wouldn't welcome me home. Once I got to town, I'd have nowhere to go. Still, it was better than the alternative. The drive there would give me time to sort things out in my head. At least, that had been my plan.

We rode for at least an hour before he pulled off and let me stretch my legs. The man really was a saint since he also bought me a drink and some food. When had someone treated me so nicely? I couldn't remember. Probably before my mom died. I didn't know his reason for helping me, and he hadn't offered an explanation. I'd put my life in his hands, and all I could do was hope I hadn't fucked up.

It took another two hours to reach the sleepy town where I'd spent most of my life, and as we drove down the main strip, I realized not much had changed. My family probably still lived in the same house. Now that we were here, I didn't know what to do. A plan still hadn't formed in my mind, and I was out of time.

"Where to?" Crow asked.

"Um, just drop me anywhere."

He stopped the bike and looked at me over his shoulder. "What the fuck, Nari? You came all the way here and don't have a place to go?"

What did it matter? He'd given me a ride, but it wasn't like he was responsible for me. We were strangers. Crow shouldn't care if I wandered the streets or not. Of course, he'd been nice enough to get me away from Gio. I should have known a decent guy wouldn't just leave me in the middle of town.

"I just needed to get this far. I appreciate everything, but I'll be fine."

"Like hell you will!" Before I could swing my leg over the bike, he took off again, forcing me to hold on tight. When he pulled up to the gates of the Hades Abyss, I wondered if I was about to find out he wasn't so nice after all. Why would he bring me here? Sure, I'd mentioned the club, but it didn't mean I was friends with any of them.

"Anyone expecting you?" the man at the gate asked.

"No, but the little one stuck to my back needs some help. Let me speak with Titan or Boomer."

"Wait here," the guy said.

Crow shook his head. "Nope. This one is a flight risk. Let me inside the gate, then make your call. I need to make sure she doesn't take off and get herself into trouble. *More* trouble."

Did he think I was twelve? I could take care of myself. Sort of. I may not have done a fantastic job so far, but it didn't mean I was a complete loser. The guy opened the gate and Crow rode through it, then stopped near what I assumed was the infamous clubhouse. I'd heard about the wild parties but never thought I'd see the place up close. Of course, it didn't exactly seem to be hopping right now. The lights were on. I heard music. However, only four bikes were parked out front. Was it too early still? Or maybe the party had already ended.

Crow patted my thigh. "Get off."

I stood and my knees nearly gave out. He gripped my arm to keep me on my feet, and I whimpered a little at the pain that shot up through my shoulder. Now that I wasn't riding behind him, I felt every single bruise and cut Gio had left on my body. This wasn't going to be a fun night.

A truck pulled up and a large man got out. I'd seen him around town before. Titan. What would he do with me? Would he kick me out? Or would he expect some sort of payment for his help? I had to wonder if I'd only traded one nightmare for another. Story of my life. Even though I hadn't heard anything about the Hades Abyss exploiting women, it didn't mean I was necessarily safe.

"What brings you here, Crow?" Titan asked.

"Got a wounded bird in need of a place to stay. Said she called this place home but wanted me to drop her off in the middle of town."

Titan came closer, eyeing me up and down. I wanted to shrink in on myself and hide from his assessing gaze. Even when he drew near enough I could feel his body heat, I couldn't bring myself to look him in the eye. At barely five feet and one hundred ten pounds, I felt like a chipmunk being stalked by a panther.

"How can this town be home if you don't actually have one to return to?" Titan asked.

"I'm not wanted there. Left a few years ago," I

said. He didn't need the details, right? It wasn't like I expected him to help me.

He reached out and tipped my face up, giving me no choice but to look at him. "Seems to me going back to your parents would be better than staying with whoever did this to you."

"Yeah, I guess you would think that." I jerked my chin free and wrapped my arms around my body before backing up a step. What did he know about it? So what if I had bruises on me? It wasn't like I'd avoid them if I went back to my dad. He might pretend like I didn't exist, but the moment someone reminded him of my presence, or Joon threw a fit and blamed me for something, he made sure I couldn't leave my room.

"How old are you?" he asked.

"Nineteen. I'm an adult, so I don't need to run home to my dad. Wouldn't matter anyway. He wouldn't let me in the door."

Titan made a low humming sound and rocked back on his heels. "Well, as a father, I have to say no matter how pissed I might be at my daughter, I'd still be grateful she came home. I'm sure he loves you, even if he doesn't always show it."

Hearing him talk about love and family annoyed me. Why did people assume all families were caring? It made me want to ask if he'd had the perfect childhood.

"I left home because I'd had enough. My family was verbally, physically, and emotionally abusive. No one was going to do anything about it, so I decided to run away. I can't say my situation improved any, but it didn't get much worse either. No offense, but don't pretend you know me or what I've been through. The fact you love your daughter is amazing, and I'm jealous of her. Want to know why?"

"Why?" he asked.

"Because my father fucking hates me. All he cares about is my stepsister and her mom. I'm just the eyesore they couldn't wait to get rid of. Didn't it occur to you if I was their precious daughter, you'd have seen my picture somewhere? I left when I was sixteen. They never fucking looked for me. What does that tell you?" I asked.

"Your family is stupid," Titan said. "Fine. I can't let you live on the streets. Since Crow brought you here, I guess we'll take responsibility for you. There's a small house you can use. And by that, I mean it's one of those tiny homes, but it has everything you'll need. Mostly."

Wait. They were giving me a house all to myself? And there wasn't a catch? As much as I wanted to hope I'd finally found a safe haven, I remained skeptical. I'd been hurt and betrayed too many times. While they hadn't said I'd have to pay for the home in any way, it didn't mean they wouldn't ask for something later. No one did something just to be nice these days.

He ran a hand over his face. "Jesus. It's too fucking late for this shit. Look, I'll show you where the place is. Get some sleep, and in the morning I'll make sure you have everything you need."

"Why?" No one ever did anything for free. What would it cost me?

"Because it's the right fucking thing to do. Come on. Get in the damn truck and I'll take you over there."

Crow patted my back gently. "You're in good hands here, Nari. I'm going to hit the road and get a little closer to home before I stop for the night. Hades Abyss will take care of you. You can trust them."

Sure, because everyone who made that claim actually meant it. That was like a serial killer convincing their victims they were safe just hours before they were chopped up into little pieces. No thanks. I refused to blindly put my trust in anyone. If my own family didn't give a shit about me, why would anyone else? But… what if he was right? The thought of having people who actually cared made warmth spread through me.

* * *

Iron

What the hell was going on? No one had noticed my presence yet. I stood in the shadows as Titan spoke with Crow. The young woman between them seemed terrified. I'd picked up bits and pieces of their conversation. So the little one needed a place to stay? I couldn't imagine anyone turning her away. I worried a strong wind might blow her over. Even in the darkness, I could see the bruises on her face.

Whoever had hurt her needed their ass beat. How could any man harm someone so fragile? I'd be willing to bet if I accidentally squeezed her wrist too hard, I'd break it. I didn't know how she'd endured the hell she'd clearly been through.

When I saw Titan force her into the truck, I waited until both he and Crow had left before getting on my bike, then I followed the President. He stopped outside one of the tiny homes. After opening the door, he ushered the woman inside, then followed her. I pulled into the driveway next to the truck and decided to make my presence known. The Pres didn't get a chance to shut the door before he heard my bike.

"What the fuck do you want, Iron?" he asked.

"She need help?" I asked.

He smirked. "Why? You offering?"

Was it so strange for me to want to lend a hand?

I'd followed the rules since coming here. It wasn't like I'd caused trouble. When I didn't answer, he shrugged and left the door open, letting me decide if I was going inside or not. The moment I crossed the threshold, the petite woman tensed. I held up my hands, showing her I meant no harm.

"My name is Iron. I only wanted to see if you needed anything," I said. Her stomach rumbled and her cheeks flushed. "I'm not a gourmet chef or anything, but I can bring a few things over and make dinner for us. If you're all right with that?"

She licked her lips and glanced from me to Titan and back, clearly not sure if she could trust me. I got it. If I were in her shoes, I'd probably feel the same way.

"What's your name?" I asked.

"Nari," she said softly.

"Pretty name. Nari, I don't have to stay. Just... make a list and I'll get whatever you need and drop it off. I doubt there's any food here, and you obviously need to eat," I said.

"All right. I just don't know why you're helping me," she said.

If I told her she looked like an angel with a broken wing, she'd probably run for the hills. Better to remain silent. She found some paper and a pen, quickly made a list of necessities, and handed it to me. The pres clapped me on the shoulder and headed out. What the hell? He wasn't going to say goodbye to her, or even make sure she had some numbers to call if she needed anyone?

Some days, the Pres really pissed me off and I wanted to call him an asshole, but I was doing my best not to make waves for the sake of my family. The blood-related ones. My club could fuck off if they were going to be dicks.

"Um. Let me write down my number, and the President's. The phone here works, so just call if something happens or you need someone. And if you're more comfortable with a woman, I can ask my sister to stop by," I said.

Her eyes widened a little. "Your sister lives here?"

"Yeah. She's actually married to someone in the club. My dad is a member too. Roe isn't the only woman here, either. Aside from you, there are four. I'm sure any of them would be glad to stop by if you wanted to talk."

She gave a slight nod. I decided to write down my sister's number, and then shot off a quick text to let her know what I'd done. It wouldn't surprise me in the slightest to find Roe over here when I got back. That was just the sort of person she was.

"I'll grab these things and be back as soon as I can. I won't just let myself in. So if you hear a knock, it's probably me." Unless it was Roe, or someone else became curious. "Oh, there's also two children in the house next to this one. One of our newest Prospects is a single dad. He's big and kind of scary looking, but I promise he won't hurt you."

"I appreciate what you and the club are doing for me. No one's been nice to me like this in a long time. In fact, I can't even remember the last time." She chewed on her bottom lip. "So… thanks."

"You're welcome." I flashed her a smile before hurrying out the door. If I didn't leave, I might be tempted to stick around for a while. For some reason, I wanted to know everything about her.

Fuck. Was this what it had been like for Roe and Pyro? I was so screwed.

Chapter Two

Nari

I'd never met anyone like Iron. While I'd felt a little hesitant when he'd first come into the house, it hadn't taken much for me to relax. There was something about him I found comforting. At first, I'd planned to ask him to leave after he dropped off the things I'd asked for. The warmth in his eyes and his easy smile changed my mind. Sure, he could have been a playboy, or completely rotten to the core. I didn't know anything about him, other than the fact he was part of the Hades Abyss and had a sister. So why did it feel like I could trust him?

He'd stayed for dinner last night, and even helped me clean up the dishes and cookware we'd used. It may have been my imagination, but he'd seemed reluctant to leave. After he'd said goodbye, I'd locked up the house and tried to settle in. Being back in this town felt strange. I'd come here voluntarily, but knowing my family would be nearby made me feel a little anxious. What would happen if I ran into any of them in town? It was bound to happen sooner or later. I couldn't hide behind these gates forever.

It hadn't occurred to me before now, but what had they told people about my absence? They hadn't declared me missing, so did their friends think I'd just gone to live with another family or something? Part of me wanted to smile over the idea of my sudden return wrecking their precious lives, and the other part felt stark terror of what my father might do to me in retaliation. The Hades Abyss had given me this place to stay temporarily, and they seemed nice. It didn't mean they would protect me when I went into town or would go toe to toe with my family. Hell, Titan might hand me over to them, since he seemed to think my father would love me and want me back. Even though I'd told him how awful my family had been, I couldn't be sure he wouldn't think I'd exaggerated everything.

How nice it would have been to belong to that sort of family! Things would have been so very different for me if any of them had actually wanted me around. I didn't remember much about the way things were before my stepmother and Joon came into the picture. I knew my mother hadn't been dead for very long before my father introduced them to me. Now that I was older, it made me wonder if he'd already been seeing her even when my mom was still alive.

If that was the case, I hoped he choked on his expensive dinners and fucking died. No, I wanted him dead regardless. People like him didn't deserve to have nice, cushy lives where others admired them. Would it even make a difference if people found out the truth? Or would they only take my father's side anyway? With money came power, and I knew my family wasn't hurting for cash.

A knock at the door startled me and I stared at it for a moment before deciding to answer. Only Iron and Titan knew I was here. While the club president scared me a little, I didn't think Iron would let him hurt me. Seeing a woman on the other side took me by surprise.

"Um, hi," I said uncertainly. Was she at the wrong place? They'd said someone lived in the house next to this one. Had she meant to go there instead?

"I'm Roe," she said, flashing me a smile. "Iron's sister. I thought I'd stop by and see if you were doing okay."

Oh. Oh! Iron had mentioned her last night. I stepped back and let her inside. She set down her purse and the bags she'd had in her hands. Maybe she'd just dropped in on her way home from the store. Either way, Iron had been right. Seeing another woman here did set my mind at ease a bit.

"Did you want something to drink?" I asked.

"I'm fine. Thank you for asking. I'm here to see if you have everything you need. Iron mentioned you gave him a list of things like shampoo, soap, and a few groceries. He told me he filled in some of the gaps."

I nodded. "He was really nice, and he stayed for dinner to keep me company."

Roe's smile widened. "Is that right? Usually my brother's like a surly bear with everyone except me. I'm glad to hear he knows how to mind his manners around other women, at least."

Iron? A surly bear? I couldn't see it, but maybe he just hadn't shown me that side of himself. It wasn't like we'd spent a lot of time together. He'd probably noticed how scared I was last night and done his best to set my mind at ease. It made me like him even more.

"Anyway, he gave me an idea of your overall size so I brought a few things for you. If anything doesn't fit, there's a receipt in the bag so you can exchange them. Although, I guess you'd need a ride. I heard someone from another club dropped you off here."

I didn't feel like getting into my story right now. "Crow saw me walking and offered me a ride. I couldn't go to my family, so…"

"The bruises on your face… do you have them elsewhere too?" she asked. "I'm not trying to be nosy. I think you may need medical attention. Iron said the way you moved made him think you'd been hurt badly."

He'd called his sister to tell her he was concerned about me? That warm feeling was back again. Why was he being so nice to me?

"I'm bruised everywhere, and I do have some cuts," I admitted.

"Would you be comfortable with a doctor coming to see you?" she asked.

"I'm not sure." When was the last time I went to the doctor? Other than routine visits, I hadn't seen anyone since we left Korea. I hadn't been permitted to go in whenever I felt sick, or when my father beat me. If anyone had seen the things he'd done to me, the government would have stepped in to do something. Or so I assumed. It's what happened on TV at any rate. Would anyone have really cared, though?

"I'd be happy to stay with you, or…" She pursed her lips. "I could call Iron. He could come stay with you while the doctor is here, but you'd have to undress enough for your wounds to be treated."

My cheeks warmed at the mere thought of Iron seeing me without all my clothes on. It wasn't like he'd be interested in a flat-chested woman like me. With his looks and sweet personality, he probably had women lining up to be with him. I couldn't picture him with someone like me.

"Hmm." Roe folded her arms. "All right. I'll have Bones drop by. He's part of the club, but he's also a doctor."

Wait. She was going to send a stranger here and leave me alone with them? My heart started to race, and I felt my palms sweat a little. What if he was scary like Titan? Or… A fist pounded on the door and I jumped, my hand going to my throat as I stared at it in terror. Was he here already?

Roe went to open it, and the moment I saw Iron, my fear began to subside. I hadn't seen her use her phone, so I didn't know why I'd assumed the doctor was here. Although, why had Iron come by right now?

"What the hell, Roe?" he demanded, shoving past her and hurrying over to me. He took my hand and tipped my chin up. "What's wrong? What did she say to you?"

"I'm fine." I licked my lips. "It was just a panic attack, I think."

"Something triggered it, and my sister is the only one here. Seriously, Roe, what the fuck did you say to her?" He turned to glare at her. I wanted to reassure him everything was fine, but my knees felt a little weak. I needed to sit before I collapsed.

"I said she should see a doctor and offered to have Bones stop by." Roe shrugged. "I didn't realize she'd react like that. You know I wouldn't hurt her, Iron. Don't be such a dick."

"Pyro is a bad influence on you. Since when do you say stuff like that?" he asked.

"Doesn't make sense for a biker to have a prim and proper wife. I needed to meet him halfway. Although, I still won't say the S or F words. There are some lines I just won't cross."

I felt like I'd been dropped into another world. What the hell were they talking about? Before I could ask, Iron turned to me again, swept me up into his arms, and carried me over to the couch. I didn't have time to freak out before he eased me down onto the soft cushions and kneeled at my feet.

"Are you sure you're okay, Nari?" he asked.

"I'm fine. Really. And she's right about me needing to see a doctor. The idea of a strange man coming in bothered me."

"No one here is going to hurt you," he said. "I promise."

"Your club didn't have to give me a place to stay,

and you didn't have to take care of me yesterday. I appreciate all of it. I'm sorry the idea of your club doctor coming here freaked me out. I haven't really had a reason to trust men."

He nodded. "I get it. A lot of women have been in similar situations. I'm amazed you let me stay as long as you did yesterday."

"I'm not scared of you," I said softly.

Roe let out a long whistle. "I never thought I'd see this day. My hard-as-nails brother, the guy who goes through women and never commits to them, the one who hates the world, is being sweet to someone other than me. She said as much, but I wasn't sure I could believe her."

"Shut the hell up, Roe!" He narrowed his eyes at her. "You're not helping the situation. Why are you here anyway?"

She nudged the bags with her toe. "Brought her some more clothes. You're welcome."

My cheeks heated again. I hadn't thought to thank her. Then again, it had been a long time since I'd felt the need to say those words. I wasn't used to so many people helping me. Or anyone at all, for that matter. It was a strange experience for me.

"She was talking to me, not you," Iron said, giving my hand a squeeze. "It seems my sister caught on rather quickly."

"What do you mean?" I asked.

He sighed and rubbed the back of his neck. "I like you, Nari. It's why I came by last night. Seeing you in the clubhouse parking lot, everything in me screamed for me to protect you. Never felt like that before. Not even with Roe. This is… different."

"You owe me and Pyro an apology," Roe said. "You can give it at our next family dinner."

Without another word, she left. I stared at the closed door for a moment before focusing on Iron again. He liked me? Why? And as what? A friend? A project? I didn't think he meant in a girlfriend sort of way.

"It's a lot, right?" he asked. "What do you need from me, Nari? Whatever it is, that's what I'll give you."

Maybe he really could help me. If I told him about my dad and the things I suffered while I lived at home, could he find a way to protect me? The idea of running into them around town terrified me. I'd rather face a million abusive men than go up against my family. Not once had I ever won against them. Even when I left, it hadn't disrupted their lives at all. If anything, they were probably glad I'd saved them the trouble of getting rid of me.

My story spilled out. The words tore free, as if they were being ripped from my very soul. At one point, Iron reached out to wipe tears off my cheeks. I hadn't even realized I was crying. I couldn't look him in the eye. What if he didn't see me the same way after this?

"They live in town?" he asked.

I nodded. "They'll eventually know I'm back. I'm sure it won't make them happy."

"First thing we need to do is find out what story they told everyone. Our club has a hacker. Wizard. I'm going to text him your name and enough information for him to look into things. Is it all right if I stay here with you? I don't feel right leaving you alone right now."

"I'd like that." Part me hoped he'd still see me the same as he did before. Or was I just some pathetic child who'd run away from home now that he knew everything?

He pulled out his phone, then shifted so he could sit beside me. He angled the screen, and I realized he was letting me read everything he was typing. Once he'd finished, he sent the message.

"I'm not sure how long it will take him. Do you want to watch a movie while we wait? Or are you hungry?" he asked.

"I don't think I could eat anything right now. A movie sounds good, though. Are you sure you don't mind staying?"

He put his arm around me, and I leaned into his side. "Even if you'd kicked me out, I'd have waited outside. I worried about you last night after I left."

"Would you... I mean... if you wanted, you could..." Why was I having so much trouble? It wasn't like I'd never shared a bed with someone before. "Do you want to stay here tonight?"

He shifted a little and I could feel him watching me. "I'm a lot older than you, Nari. You know that, right? But it doesn't mean I see you as a kid. I'm very much aware you're a woman."

"I'm glad you don't think I'm a child," I said.

"Not sure you're ready for me to stay the night. But if you'd like me to stick around until you fall asleep later, then I can do that. We've got all day. Let's watch some movies, see what Wizard has to say, then come up with a plan for dealing with your family."

"All right." It wasn't exactly the answer I'd hoped for, but I'd take it. I really didn't want to be alone right now.

I let him pick what we'd watch, and I tried to focus on the TV. My thoughts were chaotic at the moment. Fear filled me over the thought of what my father might do once he knew I was here. And I felt apprehensive. Iron seemed so wonderful, and even his sister had been nice to me. But what if the rest of the club didn't want me here? I didn't have anywhere else to go.

Iron's phone rang and he showed me the screen. *Wizard*. He paused the movie and answered the call.

"What did you find?" he asked, not even bothering to say hello first. He put the call on speaker so I could hear too. "Nari is listening as well."

"Miss Nari Kwon, it's a pleasure to meet you," Wizard said. "Just wish it were under better circumstances. Iron said you didn't know why your family never looked for you. From what I've been able to dig up, it looks like they've told everyone you're out of town."

"For all these years?" I asked.

"He said something about learning to be a proper wife." Wizard cleared his throat. "There's something else. Do you know the name Michael Sanders?"

"Yeah. His father is a friend of my dad's," I said. "What does he have to do with anything?"

"He's the one you're engaged to. Your father even put an announcement in the newspaper here last year."

I didn't understand. How could I be engaged when I hadn't even lived at home for so long? Had he known where I was all this time? It wouldn't surprise me. He could have grabbed me off the street whenever he wanted, and no one would have done anything about it.

"So you think once he realizes she's in town, there's going to be trouble?" Iron asked.

"Yeah. He'll find a way to force her back home, and most likely have her married to Sanders as quickly as possible. Looks like it's part of a business deal," Wizard said.

"Then why not use my stepsister, Joon?" I asked. "She's the favorite."

"Joon Kwon is currently dating the mayor's son. I'm sure that connection is more important to them. Doesn't mean they'll let you walk away," Wizard said. "Unless…"

"Unless what?" Iron asked.

"Unless she's not available anymore. Hard to kidnap a married woman and make her get hitched to someone else."

Iron tensed beside me. "What?"

"You heard me. Just say the word," Wizard said.

"What's going on?" I asked. "How am I supposed to get married? It's not like anyone is going to want someone like me. Even Michael Sanders… if he saw me, he'd probably dump me right away."

"First, there's not a damn thing wrong with you, Nari," Iron said. "And second… Do it, Wizard. Just tell Titan what's going on. I don't need him getting pissed at me over this shit."

"All right. Congratulations, Nari. You're now Mrs. Kaizer. Although… You know, Iron, if you wanted, I could give you the same last name as your dad."

"Not right now," Iron said.

"Wait. What's going on?" I asked. "I don't understand."

"I'll call you later, Wizard. I need to defuse the bomb you just dropped on us," Iron said. He ended the call and took a deep breath before facing me. "My name is Jack Kaizer. I go by Iron. And… the asshole who was just on the phone is going to make sure we're married. He'll hack into the government offices and make sure everything looks legit if anyone goes digging."

"Married? You and me?" I asked.

He nodded. "You can have as much time as you need to adjust to everything, but... I think you should move in with me. If you want your own room, I'll understand."

I didn't even know what to think or say. Married? To Iron? It didn't seem real.

Chapter Three

Iron

I wanted to thank Wizard, and also kick his ass. There had to have been a better way to break the news to Nari. Hell, I'd told him to go ahead and marry us without even discussing it with her first. What if she hated me for taking control? I might have done it as a way to protect her, but it didn't mean she wanted to be stuck with me for the rest of her life.

"There are some things we need to discuss," I said. "And you may not like everything I have to say."

She tipped her head to the side, waiting patiently for me to continue. I cleared my throat and glanced away for a moment. Why the hell did she have to look so damn cute? The woman was downright adorable. I'd always gone for edgy or sexy women. Nari was completely different from what I'd always thought was my *type*. I may have dated younger women, but there hadn't ever been this big of an age gap. I had no doubt we'd hear comments. As long as their words didn't hurt Nari, I couldn't care less.

"Like what?" she asked when I remained silent for too long.

"Well, I'll need to tell you how the club works. And..." Why did I find it so hard to tell her there wouldn't be a divorce? Ever. Not only would the club not allow it, I knew I would never want to let her go. "I'm afraid this is a forever sort of deal."

Her brow furrowed and her nose crinkled. "Isn't marriage supposed to be forever?"

She had a good point. Didn't mean marriages lasted these days. Then again, depending on how she'd been raised, it was possible divorce had never crossed her mind. I knew some cultures didn't only frown on divorce, but families could shun their children if they didn't stay married to their spouses.

"It is. We don't really know much about each other, so we should probably take a few days to adjust. You can ask me anything you want. But first, we need to pack your things and move you over to our home."

She smiled softly. "Our. I haven't had a home in so long. I can't wait to see what it looks like."

I only hoped she wouldn't be disappointed. The club had given me a nice place, but it was on the plain side. I hadn't bothered to decorate. On the plus side, she'd pretty much have a blank canvas. She could do whatever she wanted to the house.

I helped her gather her things, then realized I only had my bike. I wasn't ready to talk to my sister again or let my dad know I was married. *Shit.* Marauder was going to give me an earful. I hadn't been the best son, not since discovering he was my biological father. Honestly, I'd been a dick to him more often than not.

Realistically, I knew it wasn't his fault he hadn't known about me. It was a miracle I hadn't knocked someone up already. Then again, maybe I had and just didn't know. It bothered me, thinking there could be a kid out there who needed a dad while I didn't have a clue they existed. It was part of why I'd slowed down on the parties and women. Discovering my dad had been part of my club all these years, and we'd never realized we were related had made me feel like the universe shook me up and dumped me on my head.

"What's wrong?" she asked.

"Not sure how to get you and all this over to the house. We can't carry everything on my bike. Could you wait here while I borrow a club truck? We'll need to get a car or something as extra transportation for you." In fact, I could get Wizard to look into it. He might be able to hack the county impound lot records and see if there was anything we could claim. I quickly sent him a text.

Nari is going to need a vehicle. Can you help us find one?

I got a thumbs-up in response.

"Guess it's a good thing my dad let me get my license, even if it was all for show. He didn't really care if I could drive or not. He just didn't want anyone thinking something was off in our family," she said. "But I haven't driven in years."

"You can practice around the compound before going into town. I'm sure it will all come back to you." I reached out to tug her closer. "I'll be right back. Don't open the door for anyone except me. I'm not sure if Wizard has told anyone we're married."

She paled a little. "Is Titan going to be mad?"

"He's most likely going to yell quite a bit. I could tell he scared you, so I don't want you to have to face him on your own right now." If Titan intimidated her when he was being nice, I didn't want to think of how she'd react when he was pissed off. He wasn't small by any means, and my new wife seemed a bit on the timid side. Then again, considering the number of bruises I could see, it wasn't surprising. The man who was supposed to keep her safe had hurt her all her life, and it seemed like she'd found even more trouble after she'd left home.

I let myself out of the house and jogged over to the clubhouse. I snatched a set of keys behind the bar and borrowed one of the club trucks. When I pulled into the driveway at the tiny home, I saw two more bikes. Titan and Boomer were both at the front door. I got out and walked up to them, preparing myself for the worst.

"What the fuck is going on?" Titan demanded. Boomer placed a hand on his shoulder, most likely to hold him back. "Is there a reason I got a text from Wizard saying you married the girl inside?"

"I guess he didn't tell you everything," I said. "But first, could you lower your voice, Pres? You're probably scaring the shit out of Nari. You make her nervous when you aren't in a bad mood."

He took a calming breath, and seemed to be counting to ten or something, before he spoke again. "I didn't mean to scare her. And I certainly have no problem helping her out. What I need right now is for you to explain how this happened and why it's necessary, because if it's just something you wanted, then I'm going to kick your ass from one side of the compound to the other and back again."

I nodded, expecting as much. At least he was giving me a chance to tell him what was going on. I had a feeling if Boomer hadn't been here, things would have gone a bit differently. I quickly told him what Wizard discovered, and why it was necessary for Nari to be married. Although, I hadn't agreed for solely that reason.

"I like her, Titan. This wasn't a whim for me. The way Pyro knew Roe was meant to be his is exactly how I feel about Nari. I'm sorry I couldn't ask for permission. I guess on the upside, the club isn't voting anymore when we decide to claim someone as a wife or old lady. It's one less rule I've broken. I know that's how it should have gone down, but I also don't want Nari stuck inside the compound. At least our marriage will give her a layer of protection."

He nodded. "You're right, it will. I may not agree with how you handled it, but I think you did the right thing. As long as this isn't something you'll regret later."

I pointed to the truck behind me. "I'm only borrowing it to get her things over to the house. I'll drop it back by the clubhouse when we're done and come pick up my bike from here."

"I have a feeling you'll need to hold onto it for a little while longer," Titan said. "At least until you can get her a vehicle. I'll send Cam over. Load her stuff into the truck and I'll get him to drop it by your place. You can take Nari home on your bike."

Boomer flashed me a smile. "Congrats on the new wife. Although, I'd have liked to meet her. She doesn't seem like she wants to come out."

"I told her not to open the door for anyone but me, knowing she gets scared easily. Give me a second and I'll bring her out. Maybe back up a little, though?"

Boomer nodded. He and Titan both walked off a few paces, and I knocked on the door, calling out to Nari. She opened it enough to peer around the door, probably making sure it was really me. I held out my hand, and she took it, coming outside.

"I hear the two of you are married," Titan said. Nari immediately hid behind me, her hands gripping my cut. "Welcome to the Hades Abyss family, Nari. If the two of you need anything, I'm only a phone call away. I'm sure my wife will want to stop by and say hi sometime soon. Have Iron let us know when you're ready to meet more people."

She peeked around me at the President, her gaze darting over to the VP. I introduced them, and Boomer's easy smile seemed to set her at ease. I managed to put my arm around her, pulling her against my side and out from behind me.

"No one in this club will hurt you," I said. "Now

you've met the President and VP, as well as my sister. I'll introduce you to Roe's husband later, as well as my dad. Um. My dad is bigger than Titan, but you don't need to be scared of him."

I heard a shout next door, and a kid came running out. Everything happened so fast, none of us could process everything at once. Right about the time the kid's feet hit the street, I heard several bikes heading our way. I didn't get a chance to react, and neither did Titan or Boomer. Nari broke free of me and ran for the little boy, yanking him back as all three of my brothers came to a halt.

Jacob came out, terror etched on his face. His son clung to Nari for a moment, said something to her I didn't catch, and went running to his dad. The moment she saw Jacob, she paled and swayed. It seemed the bravery she'd found while saving his son had now fled. I rushed over to her.

"Nari, you're okay. That's Jacob. He's one of our Prospects, and the boy you saved is his son. Remember what I said? No one here will hurt you."

Jacob sent his son inside and came closer, moving slowly. "Thank you. He knows better than to run into the street, but his sister made him angry."

"I'm glad he's okay," she said softly.

"Jacob, this is my wife, Nari. She hasn't had the best of luck with men, so don't be offended. She's wary of everyone."

"Except you," she said, tucking her face against me.

"Right. Except me." I hugged her to me tighter. "Come on, Nari. You'll get a chance to meet everyone another day. I want to make sure you're comfortable here first."

Titan and Boomer headed over to Jacob's place

while I loaded Nari's things into the truck. She didn't have much. Since I'd bought her groceries last night, I decided to take those with us. At least I'd know I'd have something stocked she would enjoy, since she'd made the list herself. It didn't take long to empty the house, and with a quick wave to everyone, I got on my bike, then helped Nari on behind me.

Her arms went around my waist, and the way she melted against me made me wonder how many times she'd ridden on the back of a motorcycle. I wasn't sure I wanted to know the answer. What if coming here with Crow wasn't her first time? I didn't like the thought of her clinging to other men the way she was doing with me right now. Didn't matter I hadn't known her before yesterday. The caveman side of me wanted to chase off anyone who might even look her way.

"I'll go slow," I said, wondering if the ride would cause her any pain. I still didn't know how bad her wounds were. I'd need to get Bones over to the house to take a look at her. Hopefully, she wouldn't freak out when she met him.

I parked in the carport and led her through the side door and into the laundry room. She carefully took off her shoes, and I did the same. It wasn't something I'd normally do, but I'd noticed she didn't wear shoes in the house and I wondered if it was part of her culture.

"So..." I pointed to our shoes. "What's the reason behind taking off your shoes when you enter the house?"

She tensed and stared at the shoes. "Sorry. I did it without thinking."

"Nari, this is your home. I don't mind taking my shoes off. Is this part of your culture or something else?" I asked.

"In Korea, it's common to remove your shoes when you enter your home or anyone else's. It's not only a sign of respect, but we often sit and sleep on the floor. Your shoes carry a lot of dirt and germs, so we remove them."

I nodded. "All right. I'll make sure everyone is aware of the custom. Like I said, this is your home now. I don't care if you tell everyone to enter the house walking on their hands. This is *your* space, not theirs. Understood?"

"Yes." She gave me a slight smile. "Even though we moved here when I was still pretty young, my family still removed their shoes when they came home. I haven't lived in places where that was a good idea, but I guess when I came inside and saw the clean floors, instinct took over."

"Do you remember much about living in Korea?" I asked.

"Not really. I only recall a few words, but I'm not even sure if I'd say them correctly or use them in the right context. Once we moved here, my stepsister and stepmother insisted we speak only English."

"Let me show you around. The place is on the plain side, so we can change anything you don't like. Don't be afraid to tell me if you want new furniture, walls painted, or anything else."

She took my hand. "I'm glad Crow brought me here, and that I met you. I'm not sure what would have happened to me if he'd dropped me off in town like I'd asked. Either way, I couldn't have stayed where I was. The man who hurt me was going to force me into prostitution."

I tensed and tried to take a few calming breaths. The fucker was going to do what? I needed a name.

Where he lived. And then I was going to beat the shit out of him and make him wish he'd never been born. I seriously hated fucked-up guys like that. They gave the rest of us a bad name. People would often cross the street to avoid me, thinking I would hurt them. Nothing could be further from the truth. I might not have any qualms over fucking up a piece of shit like the woman who took advantage of Jacob, or the monsters hiding behind religion who'd attacked my sister, but innocent people like Nari deserved to be protected at all costs.

"Was that the first time someone has done that to you?" I asked.

"Yes. Well, sort of. I never had to work the streets or anything, but I did whatever was necessary to survive. If that meant I slept with a guy in order to not starve, then I'd do it, but I always committed to them for as long as I could. It was the only way I could feel better about myself," she said.

I heard the front door open and Cam's voice call out. "I brought the truck. Looks like there's cold stuff in the back seat."

"Take it to the kitchen," I yelled back, then led Nari farther away. I could tell she wasn't ready to meet anyone else right now. While she explored our bedroom and bathroom, I shot off a text to Titan.

Please ask everyone to knock or ring the bell if they come by my house. And from now on, everyone has to take off their shoes if they come inside.

It only took a moment to receive a *wtf* back from Titan. Yeah, I knew he probably had some questions over that last part. Not something I was going to discuss in detail right now.

It's a Korean thing. I couldn't think of an easier way to put it right now. I'd give everyone Nari's explanation later. For now, that would hopefully be enough to make sure no one came inside with shoes on.

Shit! "Cam! Don't come in with your shoes on!"

"Uh… Too late."

"Fuck," I muttered. Nari tugged on my hand. "Sorry. I didn't think to tell him. I'll clean the floors for you once he's gone."

"I can do it," she said. "This is my home now, right? Then I should take care of it."

I wasn't sure how to process her words. Did she mean she wanted to do it because she liked having a place of her own? Or was it some sort of bullshit about women being the only ones who should clean? If it was the first part, then I had no issue with her cleaning as much as she wanted. As to the second one… well, it would probably take some time for Nari to realize she wasn't my slave, wasn't beneath me in any way, and I didn't expect that sort of stuff from her.

Once Cam left, I led Nari through the rest of the house. I wondered if I could research Korean homes and find a way to bring more of her culture into our house. As she said, this was her home now. I wanted her to be at ease here and feel like she belonged. Whatever it took, I'd make sure she didn't regret being married to me.

Chapter Four

Nari

I couldn't stop wondering about the man and little boy I'd met earlier. He'd mentioned he also had a daughter. How did the three of them manage to live in such a small home? When Iron had said the club had women and children, I hadn't thought much of it. Not until I'd met Roe and the little boy. Hearing there were families here and seeing it were two different things. Even though his son had run into the street, the man had only been worried about him. He hadn't yelled at the boy, hit him, or threatened him in any way.

"You're deep in thought," Iron said.

"Things are just so different here. If I'd run into the street when I was younger, my father would have made sure I couldn't even walk by the next day. Of course, he wouldn't have done that in front of anyone." I hadn't considered that. What if that man hurt the boy once they were home? "Will the little boy be okay?"

Iron ran a hand down my back. "He'll be fine. Jacob is never harsh with his children. In fact, he got into some trouble when he tried to save his daughter. It's how he came to be part of the club. He suffered a traumatic brain injury, and it can't be cured. Jacob used to be an MMA fighter. Got hit one too many times. He didn't get proper medical care at the time, and unfortunately, his condition is now irreversible."

"He seemed nice," I said.

"He is. He protected my sister when people abducted her. If it weren't for Jacob, we may not have gotten to Roe in time. He also stepped in to help our club when it counted. In exchange, we got his daughter the help she needed, and offered him that home and the chance to prospect for the club."

"What exactly does that mean?" I asked.

"A Prospect is someone who does a lot of the grunt work around here. They have to prove themselves, and their loyalty, before they can earn a patch and road name. I don't see any issues with Jacob patching in when the time is right."

"And the one who brought the truck? Cam, I think was his name?"

Iron nodded. "Cam is also a Prospect. There's one more. Mason."

"It sounds like there are a lot of people who live here." Would I ever be able to remember everyone's names? I worried I'd feel overwhelmed when I got a chance to meet them all. "And there are more kids?"

"There are, and yeah, the club is growing. My dad and I came here somewhat recently. If it weren't for my sister marrying Pyro, we'd still be in Missouri. When she decided to make a life for herself here, Titan offered us both a place with this chapter." He tucked my hair behind my ear. "I'm damn glad about that right now. Otherwise, I might never have met you."

I could tell there was something else he wanted to say. He'd been a little tense ever since the tour of the house. Had I not made it clear I liked the place? Was he worried I didn't want to stay here? Or was something else weighing on his mind?

"I feel like there's something you aren't saying." I reached up to place my hand over his, where he'd laid it to rest against my neck. "Whatever it is, please don't keep it from me. I've already lived a life full of lies and misconceptions. I don't want to do that anymore."

"I wasn't sure how to bring up the club doctor. I'd like for him to take a look at you, but I didn't think you'd feel comfortable. We could find a female doctor in town."

I shook my head. I wasn't ready to venture out there yet. Not after hearing what my father had done. No good would come of him knowing my current location. Eventually, I'd have to see him. When I felt ready.

I knew Iron had married me to keep me safe. However, they didn't know my father and what he was capable of. I still worried it wouldn't be enough to save me.

"I'm fine with Bones," I said. "Just... stay with me?"

He nodded. "I'll hold your hand the entire time if that's what you want. You going to be okay partially undressing in front of us?"

"You're my husband now, right?"

"That doesn't mean you should offer yourself to me, unless it's something you really want. I'm not like that, Nari. You can ask anyone around here. Some will say I'm an ice-cold bastard, but they'll all agree I don't take advantage of women."

I couldn't see the "ice-cold" part. It wasn't the first time someone had made a comment about him acting differently with me. Was it true? Was I only seeing one side of him? It made me feel a little apprehensive. It was possible I'd only traded one abuser for another, although Iron didn't seem like the sort to do something like that. We were still strangers, though, and I couldn't say with any certainty things wouldn't go badly for me here.

I hoped the more I got to know him and the others in the club, the better I'd feel. Right now, I might be back in a town I'd lived in most of my life, but being at the Hades Abyss compound was like living in an entirely different world.

"Never thought you did," I said. "And I can't say for sure when I'll be ready for sex, but I do want to sleep next to you at night. If I hide in another room, it will only make it more difficult for us to grow closer, won't it?"

"You make a good point. But again, at your pace, and only when you're ready." He leaned down and kissed my cheek. His lips felt warm, and I couldn't help but smile. No one had ever been so sweet to me before. Even if this was all a charade, I'd enjoy it while I could. And I'd keep my fingers crossed the Iron I was getting to know was the real one. I knew there was a chance he was showing me his true self.

"Do you and your sister get along? There seemed to be some tension between you earlier."

His eyebrows rose. "Changing the subject?"

"Not entirely. She'd offered to stay with me before when the doctor came, but I hadn't felt comfortable enough with her. It made me remember the way you'd acted with her at the other house."

"I didn't know about Roe until a year ago. That being said, I love my sister. I'd take down anyone who ever tried to hurt her. At the same time, I didn't like the fact she'd scared you. I don't think it was intentional. She's not the type to hurt someone."

So, in other words, typical brother-sister dynamic. Or the way I thought it should be. When it came to siblings, I didn't exactly have the best example with Joon. I only wished we had that sort of relationship. Instead, she'd done everything she could to destroy my life.

"Do you think Roe and I could be friends?" I asked.

"If I know my sister half as well as I think I do, then she already considers you family. The simple fact

I was interested in you would have been enough for her to decide you're one of us. Now that we're actually married, she'll claim you as a sister."

Tears stung my eyes. Really? Someone actually wanted me as their sister? I couldn't imagine such a thing. When I'd first met Joon, I'd been happy, thinking I'd have someone who wanted to hang out with me. Instead, I'd ended up with a spoiled monster who hated my guts. I still didn't know why she disliked me so much. I'd never done anything to her.

"Go ahead and call Bones," I said. "I'd rather get this out of the way, but I'm warning you, it won't be pretty. Not only because of my current wounds, but I have some scars as well."

"Nari, I'm not going to see you any differently. The things other people have done to you don't detract from who you are as a person, and I can tell you're sweet. You may have fought hard to stay alive, but I can see the gentleness inside you. Hell, you looked like a terrified rabbit when faced with Titan last night. Why would some marks on your skin change anything?"

I understood what he meant. While I should have felt relieved at his words, I didn't. Even if he didn't see me differently, I couldn't look at them without thinking there must be something wrong with me. Why else would everyone have hurt me all my life?

"Hey." He gently touched my cheek. "Whatever dark thoughts you just had, shake them loose. I meant what I said. Put those things in your past and leave them there. I'm not going to let anyone hurt you again, Nari. You're my wife. Do you honestly think I'd stand by while someone hit you, or verbally abused you? Because I won't. I'll make them wish they were dead."

If this was his way of reassuring me, I had to

admit it was rather unique. I'd never had anyone threaten someone for me before. It felt… good. Would he really harm someone? I'd heard the whispers around town about the Hades Abyss. While they weren't obvious about it, people said they broke the law on a regular basis. I'd never really considered what that might mean. Drugs. Guns. Prostitution. Murder?

The thought of being part of a club that might do those things should terrify me. Instead, I only felt grateful Iron would stand by my side no matter what. Of course, it could all be a lie. For some reason, I felt like I could believe him. I'd been lied to so many times, I hoped by now I could spot those who intended to betray me. He seemed different from the others. Men had promised to help me, smiled at me with warmth and kindness, only to want things in return. I'd learned the hard way nothing was ever free.

Even those who dated me weren't honest about their intentions. They used me, plain and simple. And every last one of them was seeing other women. My life had been filled with liars even before I ran away. People at school always said one thing to my face, but I heard them whispering to others behind my back. People were devious and didn't seem to care about others.

"Will I ever fit in here?" I asked.

"What makes you think you don't already?"

He made a good point. I'd only met a few people. While Roe had seemed bubbly and bright, maybe the other women were more reserved or shy. I'd try to do better and not think so negatively about myself, but I knew it would take time. After years of being told how worthless I was, I knew it wouldn't be easy to crawl out of the hole. Iron had given me an opportunity to figure out who I was, and who I wanted to be.

"I guess I'll find out sooner or later," I said. "But first, ask Bones to come over. You seem worried about me."

"I am. Put your things away while I make my call. There should be enough room, but if not, just shove my stuff to the side. Remember, Nari, this is your home now."

I nodded and watched him walk away. It didn't take long to put up the few clothes I had. Even with my belongings mixed in with his, there was still space left over. While I might not have a large wardrobe, it appeared Iron didn't either. He had one drawer with socks and underwear. One full of T-shirts, and the bottom one had three pairs of sweatpants and nothing else. The closet only contained a few pairs of jeans and two button-down shirts.

He'd mentioned he hadn't lived here for long. Did he still have things in Missouri, or did he not own a lot of clothes? It looked sparse to me. For the first time ever, I wondered what it would be like to shop for someone else. Something told me it would be a little thrilling to pick out things for Iron. Whenever he wore something I'd chosen, it would make me feel special.

One step at a time, Nari. We didn't know nearly enough about one another. He might not be the type of man who enjoyed someone buying clothes for him. If that was the case, then I'd have to hide my disappointment.

I didn't know how much time passed before someone knocked on the bedroom door. I glanced over and saw Iron and another man behind him. He carried a black bag in his hands, just like the ones I'd seen doctors carry on TV. Which meant he was Bones.

"Nari, are you still up for this?" Iron asked.

"Let's get it over with. What do I need to do?" I

asked.

"Nothing yet. Well, maybe sit on the edge of the bed. I'm going to listen to your heart, check your ears, and all that good stuff. We'll start with some basics. I'm sure you've already figured it out, but I'm Bones. Legally, I'm Dr. Masters."

"It's nice to meet you," I said. "I'm Nari Kwon."

Iron cleared his throat. "No. You're Nari Kaizer."

"Right." My cheeks warmed. "Sorry. It may take me a little bit to get used to that."

I sat down and let the doctor check my temperature, blood pressure, listen to my heart and lungs, and he even looked at my eyes and ears. He backed up several steps and eyed me carefully.

"The bruises on your arms and face... where else do you have them?" he asked.

"Everywhere. The night I left, I'd been beaten. They were going to force me into being one of their whores. I decided to leave instead."

Bones folded his arms. "Good girl. You made the right decision. I know Iron will take care of you. Would you be all right with me drawing some blood? I'd like to do a basic workup so I'll have a baseline. If I'm going to be your doctor, I'd like to have as much information as I can. Iron said you hadn't been to a doctor in a long time."

"My dad made sure I got all the vaccines I needed. Other than that, I wasn't allowed to go to the doctor."

"Probably afraid someone would notice the abuse you suffered," Bones said.

I knew that's what it was. If anyone had found out, my father would have been ruined. He'd do anything to protect his image. Even tell everyone his runaway daughter was engaged to someone and would return when the time was right. It still bothered me. Had he known where I was? How else would he hand me over to my fiancé?

I took a breath to steady my nerves, then pulled my shirt over my head. Bones and Iron both tensed as they stared at me. I looked away, unable to hold either of their gazes. Being flat-chested meant I never needed a bra, and I wasn't wearing one now. I heard a growl, then found myself covered with a blanket.

"What the fuck, Nari? You didn't tell me you'd be completely naked." I glanced up at him and noticed the way he glared at Bones. The poor doctor looked both amused and embarrassed.

"Not anything I haven't seen before, Iron, and you know I'm only looking at her as a physician and not as a man."

"I don't give a fuck! She's my wife. There are parts of her only I should see."

Was it wrong I wanted to laugh? For a big, tough biker, sometimes he sounded so cute. Like now.

"I'm okay, Iron. Like he said, he's a doctor. You wanted to make sure I was all right, and this is part of it."

"No. I changed my mind. I'll tend to any wounds you have."

Bones pressed his lips together, and I could tell he was close to laughing. He cleared his throat. "All right. Nari, put your shirt back on. I'll draw your blood, and then I'll leave the two of you alone. Results should be in within a few days. I know this is a sensitive question, but should I also run a test for STDs or pregnancy?"

"I'm not a virgin, if that's what you mean. There's no way I'm pregnant, though. I haven't had sex with anyone in months. I'd have known by now."

"Regular periods?" he asked.

"Yeah. I mean, I haven't missed any. They're never exactly on time, but I haven't been more than a few days late and sometimes it's early."

"Then we can skip the pregnancy test. I still want to check for STDs just to be safe, and um… at the risk of Iron kicking my ass, I think the two of you should hold off on being intimate until we know for sure you're clean."

"Run mine too," Iron said. "I haven't been tested recently. I'm not letting her do this shit alone."

"All right. Have a seat next to her."

It didn't take Bones long to draw our blood and fill the various vials. I didn't know how he'd thought to have them prepped and ready to go, or maybe he'd just tried to be ready for anything. Either way, I hoped everything came back okay. For both of us.

"I'll call with results when I get them. Congratulations on your marriage, and welcome to the family, Nari. I think you're going to like it here."

Bones left, and Iron took my hand. I leaned into his side. Was this what it had been like for Joon all these years? To have someone supportive and understanding? It was my turn now. One way or another, I'd get my happy ending! I was done giving up on everything I wanted.

"You and me against the world, Nari. Whatever you need, it's yours," he said.

"I think… all I'll need is you. Sounds corny, doesn't it? But it's the truth. You've given me something I haven't had in so long I'd forgotten what it felt like."

"What's that?" he asked.

"Hope. You've given me hope, Iron."

"Call me Jack," he said. "At least when we're

alone."

"Jack… Are you sure you won't regret agreeing to this? I'm sure you could have had any woman you wanted. I'm not beautiful. Certainly not curvy. There's not a single thing I'm good at."

"Hey. We talked about this. No more negative thoughts, Nari. I happen to think you're adorable, and yes, I find you beautiful. I don't care if you're an A-cup or your tits are so big you need help carrying them around. As long as they're yours, I'll love them. So stop worrying over nonsense."

"I'll do my best." That was as much as I could promise for now.

Chapter Five

Iron

I had a wife, a woman to hold every night, and I had to keep my dick in my pants. The old me would have been pissed. Since finding out about Roe, and seeing her with Pyro, I'd changed. I didn't care about easy pussy and wanted something lasting. With Nari, I could have that. It just required me to be a little patient. I vaguely remembered someone saying something about the best things in life requiring a little effort. "I'm proud of you," I said. "I'd expected you to be more afraid of Bones."

I slowly undressed her, amazed she actually let me. When the last garment fell to the floor, I walked around her, assessing every bruise, scrape, and scar. It wasn't as bad as I'd feared, but worse than I'd hoped. Not only was her frame petite but I could tell it had been a while since she had eaten regular meals. Her hip bones and ribs were more pronounced than they should be. No matter how much I tried to hold back, I couldn't. I stepped closer and wrapped her in my arms, holding her close.

She didn't stiffen or tense in any way. The simple fact she was willing to let me hold her like this showed how much she trusted me. If there was some way to ease her pain or take away her scars, I would. It didn't matter if I saw her as beautiful. I wanted her to be able to see herself that way, and right now, I could tell she didn't.

"Will you get in the shower with me?" she asked. "I know we can't do anything, and I don't think I'm ready for that anyway, but I want to see how I react. I've always shut off part of my mind and did whatever was necessary, and I don't want that to happen when we're together."

"Whatever you need, you can have." I released her and took a few steps back. I removed my cut and set it on the counter. So far, she didn't seem scared. Of course, I was still dressed. I did my best not to make it obvious I was watching her, but if I saw even the slightest hesitation on her part, I'd stop. By the time I'd removed the rest of my clothes, she'd wrapped her arms around her waist and chewed on her bottom lip. I could feel her gaze on me. She might have scars, but so did I, and a lot of ink.

She let out a breath and gave a brisk nod before turning to the shower. I reached over to turn it on, then let her set the temperature to something comfortable for her. Nari went into the shower stall and soaked her hair. When she glanced my way, I took it as permission to join her. Despite the fact she'd asked to shower with me, it didn't mean she was truly ready for something like this. I wasn't going to take the initial invitation to mean I had a greenlight to get in here with her.

"If you feel like you're going to panic, or change your mind, just tell me," I said. "I won't promise to always make you happy and give you a perfect life. It sounds like an unreasonable thing to say. I'm going to screw up sometimes. But I will do my best to make sure you have the things you need, to show you I care about you, and stay by your side regardless of what chaos lands in our path."

She sighed. "How are you single?"

"Huh?" My brow furrowed. Where the hell did that come from?

"You're amazing, Iron."

"Jack," I corrected. "It's just us right now."

"Right. Jack. I mean it, though. You say all the right things, treat me well, you're gentle when you touch me and try not to move too quickly so you won't scare me. Women had to have been throwing themselves at your feet."

"None of them were the right one," I said. "I won't lie and say I gave them a fair chance. Some of them may have been good women who genuinely liked me. Most were just chasing a biker for a good time. My past isn't pretty, Nari."

"Neither is mine. If you aren't going to hold mine against me, why should I hold yours against you?"

She made a fair point. However, from what I'd observed, women had a tendency to want a man who knew what he was doing in the bedroom without thinking about the women he'd been with to learn those skills. As much as I wanted to pretend I'd never been with anyone but her, she needed to know who I really was. The man she saw before her wasn't the same one I showed the rest of the world. My sister was probably the only one who'd had a glimpse of my softer side, and even then, it wasn't nearly the same.

"Want me to wash your hair?" I asked.

She gave a slight nod and turned. Her back had just as many scars and bruises as her front, and I really wanted to kill the assholes who'd done this to her. Especially the one she'd recently run from, and her father. I needed to know more, and at the same time, I worried it would be too traumatizing for her to talk about it. She probably needed not only a doctor but a therapist. Would she agree to see one? Probably not. Nari had spent her entire life running from her problems. I didn't think she was ready to face them just yet.

I massaged her scalp as I worked the long strands of her hair into a lather. With the right care, I imagined it would feel silky. Right now, it felt a little dry and brittle. I didn't know much about what women needed for their hair. Thankfully, I'd been able to ask someone at the store and I'd not only bought her shampoo, but also conditioner and something called a hair mask.

I held up both containers. "Which do you want to use today?"

She took them from me and read the labels, then handed the mask to me. I helped her rinse her hair before saturating it with the thick cream. When it came time to wash her body, I hesitated. Closing my eyes, I took a breath and held it for a moment. If I did this, and ended up getting hard, she might never trust me again. Could I touch her without my body reacting?

"What's wrong?" she asked.

"Worried how you'll react if I get hard," I admitted.

"Oh." Her eyes widened a little, and she glanced down at my cock.

Great. It twitched as she stared. The longer her gaze remained on me, the more difficult it became to remain soft. She reached out and her fingers lightly grazed my shaft, and I knew there was no way I could hold back. My dick got hard in an instant, and I immediately took a step back. Shit.

"Nari, that isn't a good idea," I said. "I'm not going to force myself on you or anything. That's not something you ever have to be afraid of. Not with me."

"You enjoyed that though, right?" she asked.

"It was brief, but yeah... Clearly, I got turned-on." Why the hell was she torturing me like this? I was doing my best to be good, to give her the time and space she needed, and I sure the fuck didn't want her thinking this was a requirement. We were married.

Sure, most couples had sex. Didn't mean we had to. Not right now, and not ever if that wasn't something she ever desired. My hand worked just as well as sticking my dick into random pussy.

"Bones said we shouldn't have sex, and I'm assuming that means I can't put you in my mouth either." *Holy fuck!* Yeah, she was definitely trying to kill me. "Can I still touch you? I could make you come with my hand, if that's okay."

"Why?" My voice sounded more like the pathetic croak of a frog. This pint-sized woman was turning me inside out.

"I want to. You're the only man who hasn't asked for sexual favors or demanded anything of me. It's nice being able to offer you something without any sort of expectations." She wrapped her arms around her waist. "Makes me feel almost normal. Like we're just a regular couple."

Aw, hell. I pulled her into my arms, doing my best to ignore my cock. "We *are* a regular couple, Nari. Did we meet the way most people in town do? No. But I've learned that when it comes to my club and the women they choose, each situation is unique and far different from what any of us expected. I'm still learning about the men at this chapter, but I can give you some examples from Missouri."

"Like what?" she asked.

"Spider was the President there until not too long ago. His woman is young enough to be his granddaughter. Her father let men use her, prostituted her, and abused her worse than what you've experienced. Her first day at the club, she stripped naked and offered herself to him, thinking she was there to be a whore for the club. He was pissed as hell about the situation, and I think it broke him a little to see her like that. I get it now, even if I didn't back then."

"So my father isn't the only monster," she murmured.

Sadly, no, he wasn't. There were too many bastards out there who had no business claiming the title of *Dad*. Same for women, though. Jacob's kids had the worst mother ever. She'd taken advantage of Jacob.

"Spider's woman had two sisters. One came to our club with her. She's with Rocket now. Same thing. She misunderstood why she was there and offered herself to him. Except she was only sixteen at the time. He ran to his bedroom and locked the door." Nari snickered a little. Even I could admit it was funny, and yet it wasn't. "Fox's woman also suffered sexual abuse. Her dad is a biker too, and he asked us to save her. Raven didn't trust anyone except Fox. They ended up together. Think he fell for her the second he saw her."

"You said your sister was kidnapped. Did they…"

I shook my head. "No, she didn't have to suffer anything like that. At least, not then. Another club hurt her, though. They spiked her drink, and my brother's. Cotton didn't have any idea what was going on and thought Roe was willing. He did everything he could to make things right, but she refused and ended up moving here to start over. She doesn't really remember much from that night."

"You said there are others here. Are their stories anything like mine?" she asked.

"Let's finish washing up and get out. The water will get cold. We can talk more over some food." Now that I'd had time to get myself under control, I thought I might be able to touch her without feeling like a complete ass. But Nari had other ideas. She pulled away from me, and reached for the soap, rubbing the bar between her small hands. "What are you doing?"

Without a word, she reached for my dick, wrapping her fingers around the shaft. I sucked in a breath and backed into the shower wall. She followed, not letting go. I kept my gaze focused on her face as she stroked me. The second it looked like she was forcing herself to do this, I'd put a stop to it. Until then... Well, I could tell her no, but for some reason, she seemed to want this. Or maybe she needed to do it. A way to prove to herself she had control of her life again? Whatever the case, it wasn't a hardship for me.

Her grip had just the right amount of firmness, and the little twist she added on each downstroke made my balls draw up. It had been quite a while since a woman touched me, and I knew it wasn't going to take much for her to get me off. She glanced up, and the moment our gazes locked, I was done. I felt a tingle in my spine and came so hard my cum splattered all over the front of Nari.

It took a second to catch my breath. "Are you okay?"

"Yeah." She lifted her hand and stared at it.

I saw I'd made a mess of more than just the front of her. Reaching for the soap, I helped her clean up. After what she'd just done, I wished she'd say something more. Shouldn't have let her do this. No matter how amazing it felt, I should have stopped her. I'd known she wasn't ready, no matter what she said. Whatever happened to her, it was enough to make come back here, to a place she'd hated and a family she feared.

"I'm sorry," I said.

"For what?"

"Everything." I cupped her cheek. "Why don't

we get dressed and I'll make something for us to eat? If you want, we can watch a movie afterward, or we can figure out what else you need and make a list."

"You've already given me so much."

"Not nearly enough. For one, you're going to need more clothes and shoes. And second, you need to make this place your home. We can shop online if you aren't ready to go into town just yet."

She gave a slight nod, and we finished up in the shower. Once we were dressed, I led her to the kitchen. I needed to feed her before we did anything else. The woman was skin and bones. Judging by her overall size, she'd never carry much weight on her, but I did want to help her get healthy again. It was clear the bastard who hurt her hadn't given a shit if she starved to death or not.

Sooner or later, I'd get a name from her. If she wouldn't tell me where he was, then I'd ask Crow what town he'd been in when he picked her up. Once I knew that, I'd have one of the hackers locate the asshole. I'd make sure he never hurt another woman. There was a special place in hell for men like him, and I was more than happy to send him there.

I made soup and sandwiches for us and took stock of the items I had in the kitchen. I'd need to either place an order and get a Prospect to pick it up or run to the store myself.

"What kind of things do you like to do?" I asked as we sat down to eat.

"I'm not sure what you mean."

"Well, some of the women here like to read. I saw one drawing one day. Is there anything like that you enjoy?"

"I always liked books," she said. "It gave me an escape from reality. I'm not sure if I'd be good at anything like drawing. Although, I always wanted to learn how to play the piano."

"We can get one," I said. Not that I had any fucking clue how much one would cost. Didn't matter. If she wanted one, I'd figure it out. There were always jobs I could volunteer for if I needed extra cash. Titan was good about making sure everyone was taken care of. I'd offered to help with the strip club, but now that I had a wife, I wasn't sure how I felt about it anymore. Would she be understanding about a job like that?

"What's wrong?" she asked.

"Just thinking about all the things we don't know about each other. Like my job. Not sure you'll like it."

"What is it?" she asked.

"I help run the strip club. It's a new venture for us, and since it was sort of my idea, I help manage the place. But it means I'm around mostly naked women on a regular basis. You're my wife now, Nari. I don't want to do anything to make you uncomfortable. If you want me to do something else, I'll ask Titan to move me. Plenty of the guys here would love to take my spot."

She shook her head. "It's okay. It's just work, right?"

"Exactly. I'm not sleeping with them or anything. Never touch them."

"Then I don't see a problem with it, unless you've forced them to do that kind of work."

"No. They aren't coerced into it. It's a good-paying job, and a lot of them either need the cash to take care of their families or they're saving up so they can go to college."

She tipped her head to the side and studied me. Did she dislike women who worked as strippers? Or was something else on her mind? The silence bothered me. I couldn't tell how she felt about my job, or the strip club in general.

"A lot of women don't have many options," she said. "I'm assuming your club keeps them safe?"

"Of course we do!"

"Then I think you should keep working there. It doesn't bother me, Jack. Not even a little."

I reached across the table and took her hand. How many women would be so understanding? More than once, I'd heard people around town talk about the strippers, making it sound like they were somehow less than everyone else. I didn't understand why it mattered how they earned their money. It was an honest job, paid well, and some of them were really good dancers. As long as they were fine with what they did, everyone else needed to fuck the hell off.

"I'm glad you feel that way," I said. "Come on. Let's figure out what else you need and order some stuff."

I led her to the living room and grabbed my laptop off the coffee table. Shopping might be more fun for her in an actual store, but this would do for now. Once she had all the basics, and a few extras, maybe she'd be ready to leave the compound. If not, we'd buy more stuff and have it delivered. Whatever Nari needed, I'd see she had it.

Chapter Six

Nari

Why had he worried about my reaction to his job? It wasn't like he was breaking the law or forcing those women into prostitution. Sometimes people really baffled me. *Wait.* Had he thought it would bother me for him to work around strippers? I could see how some women might feel odd about their husband seeing naked women every day. Considering the life I'd led since leaving home, it wasn't a big deal for me. If a man was going to cheat on a woman, it didn't matter where he worked... He'd find a way if that was what he really wanted to do.

However, if I were to visit him while he was working and caught him getting off while watching them, or getting a lap dance, then it might bother me. Especially after we'd been together for a while. So far, Iron didn't seem like the type of man to do something like that. We were married now. There wasn't any point in him putting effort into getting me to trust him, unless he really meant what he was saying. At least, that's what I kept telling myself. My past made it hard for me to listen even to my own reassurances.

My first day in my new home hadn't gone quite the way I'd expected. Iron not only treated me with respect, but I could tell how hard he was trying to help me feel secure. People had knocked on the door twice, and he'd sent them away. We'd spent the entire day talking and watching movies, or shopping online. He'd seemed really bothered by the fact I hadn't wanted to decorate, so I'd given in and selected an area rug online. Someone from the club picked it up and dropped it off at the house last night, and now it covered part of the living room floor. I had to admit I liked the splash of color.

"I know your life at home was far from ideal. Do you ever want kids? Or is that a hard no?" he asked as he took a swallow of coffee.

I pressed a hand to my belly. I hadn't even thought about the fact he might want to be a dad one day. With all the scars on my body, he hadn't asked about each individual one, and neither had Bones. I stood and lifted the hem of my shirt, pointing out a two-inch scar along my lower belly.

"This is a stab wound," I said. "My first year on the streets, I got caught up in a fight. Someone stuck a knife in me. I probably would have bled out, but a nurse was walking nearby when it happened. She managed to get me to a place that patched me up with no questions asked."

"I'm assuming this relates to you having children."

I nodded. "It went in pretty deep. The person who stitched me back together warned me I may not be able to have children. I've never had anyone look at it since then, and I haven't been tested for fertility, obviously. There's a chance I can't have babies."

"If you can't, we'll adopt. Only when or if you decide you want kids. It's not a deal breaker for me, Nari. The children around this place are cute, and I like seeing them play outside. Not sure I'm really dad material, though."

I felt a little relieved. "So, do *you* want babies?"

"Only if you do." He smiled a little. "That one is entirely up to you. If you never want children, I'm fine with it just being the two of us from now until eternity. Or if baby fever kicks in, then we'll figure it out then. My sister is pregnant. No reason we can't just be a doting aunt and uncle."

No one had ever asked if I wanted a family. Until now. Hearing him say he was fine either way set me at ease. I'd never really been the type to want to raise a bunch of kids. Or even one, for that matter. I'd always been living day-to-day, never knowing where I'd be or what would happen next. This was the first time I could seriously sit down and contemplate what my future would look like.

"I dropped out of school," I said. "Does it bother you I never finished high school or got my GED?"

He twisted his cup in his hands and stared at me. Had I said something wrong? Would I ever get to know him well enough to understand the different looks he had throughout the day? Instead, I was always left wondering what was going on inside his head when he did something like this. Which seemed to be often.

"The question you need to ask is whether or not it bothers *you*. I accept you as you are, Nari. If not completing high school is something you don't like about yourself, then I'll help you prepare for the GED."

"And if it doesn't bother me, but only makes me feel like other people are judging me for it?"

He leaned forward. "Then tell them to fuck off because it's your life and your decision. It doesn't matter what anyone else thinks. Not even me."

Were all older men like this? Sure, I'd been with guys who weren't my age. Just not any as old as Iron. How much had he seen and done in his lifetime already? Did I come across as a child to him? No, wait. He'd just said no one's opinion mattered except mine. I needed to stop wondering what he liked or didn't like about me, or how he saw me.

"Are you trying to say the only one who can make me feel inferior is myself?" I asked.

He pointed to me. "Bingo! If you allow what others think to influence how you see yourself, it's only going to set you up for a miserable life. Learn to love who you are, Nari. Do you even realize how strong you are? Look at everything you've been through, and yet here you are, still alive and ready to fight if necessary."

He wasn't wrong. I'd never seen myself as being strong, but maybe I was. The fact men had always been able to hurt me had made me feel weak. In time, I hoped I could be someone who could stand proudly by his side.

"You said your dad lives here too, right?" I asked.

"He does. We both moved here to be close to Roe. Did you want to meet him?"

The way he asked made me pause. "Is he... not like you? I mean, is he scary like Titan?"

"Hmm. Not an easy question to answer. For some people, my dad can be truly terrifying. With you, he'll do whatever it takes to make you feel welcome. He's big, though. Like Titan. Actually, he used to be even broader, but as he's aged, I think he's started to shrink a little. Don't tell him I said that, or he'll come out swinging."

I couldn't help but smile. It seemed like they had a good relationship. "I wish my dad had been more like yours. It sounds like your family is really close."

Iron choked on his next swallow of coffee. "Excuse me?"

"You aren't?"

"Uh, no. Well, we weren't. Marauder and I have grown closer since coming here to be with Roe. Before this... Let's just say I didn't handle it well when I found out he was my dad. I had no fucking clue until about a year ago. Roe and I found out at the same time we were related and had the same dad. Our moms are different, though."

"Did he not know he had kids?" I asked.

"No. Neither woman told him they were pregnant. Can't really blame him for not being part of our lives, but it still pissed me off at the time. We still have moments when we clash. Not as bad as before."

"Would it be okay to invite your family over? I already met Roe. She's married though, isn't she? I think she mentioned that, or you did. And there's your dad… I think knowing more people will help me settle in more. I'm just not ready to meet the entire club."

He pulled his phone from his pocket and set it on the table, then dialed someone and put it on speaker.

"Everything okay?" a man asked when the call connected.

"Your daughter-in-law would like to meet the family." Iron smirked when his dad coughed and sputtered on the other end of the line. "I'm going to text Roe in a minute. Why don't we plan on having lunch together?"

"Wait. Daughter-in-law? What the fuck did you do, Iron?" he asked.

"Got married, obviously. You're getting slow in your old age."

"You little shit." He huffed. "I'll be there, and then you're going to explain how you're married when no one even knew you were seeing anyone."

"Roe already met her," Iron said. "Bye… Dad."

He hung up before the man could say anything else, then threw back his head and laughed like a lunatic. What the hell had I just gotten myself into?

"What was that?" I asked.

"I threw my sister under the bus. Dad will call

- 65 -

her all pissed off that he's the last one to know, then he'll remember she's pregnant and treat her like she's made of glass. Should prove to be entertaining."

They were nuts. Clearly. So why did I feel a little jealous over the interaction between Iron and his dad? He may say they'd had some conflict between them, but I could hear the affection in both their voices. My father had never spoken to me like that. At least, not as far back as I could remember. Maybe he had when my mom had still been alive. It was so long, everything from that far back was a blur. I didn't even remember what my mother looked like, or the sound of her voice.

"We only have four chairs at the kitchen table. Where is everyone going to sit?" I asked.

"Good point. Hold that thought." He called someone and I assumed it was his father based on the conversation, even though I could only hear Iron's side. "Bring a chair with you. We'll need an extra at the table."

He hung up immediately after. "That was rather rude."

"We're family. What's he going to do?"

Yep. Definitely his dad, then. I hadn't thought he'd speak like that to Roe. Even though they'd argued yesterday, I could tell he loved her. If Joon and I could fight like regular siblings, maybe I wouldn't have suffered so much. Instead, I ended up with an evil stepsister and stepmother... and both turned my father into a monster. Unless he'd always been one and I hadn't realized it.

"Do we have enough stuff to feed everyone?" I asked.

"Well, I was going to make it for dinner one night, but it's going to be lunch now. The large package of chicken needs to be cut into small chunks.

I'll season it and cook it in a skillet. Think you can help with the veggies and rice?"

"What do I do with them?"

"Slice the peppers and onions into thin strips and sauté them. I got a box of minute rice, so it's quick and easy to make. Once the veggies and chicken are finished, we'll mix them together and serve them over the rice. You're okay with spicy stuff, right?"

I blinked at him. "I love spicy food. Even though my stepmom and Joon wanted to embrace all things American when we moved, my dad would still require us to eat at least one Korean meal a week. My favorite was *Bibim Guksu*, which is a spicy noodle dish."

"Was that the only part of your heritage you were able to hold onto?" he asked.

"Pretty much. Although my father clearly held onto the belief a woman's family should arrange a marriage for her. I'd be willing to bet he set up Joon with the mayor's son. He wouldn't want to give up any of his power, even if he does dote on her."

"Whenever we run into them in town, I make no promises to mind my manners. I might very well put my fist through his face."

I'd almost pay to see my father's reaction. Then again, considering Iron's build, he'd probably knock my dad out cold. Now I *really* wanted to see it happen. There'd been plenty of times I wished I could cause him even a fraction of the pain he'd put me through. Others, I'd have given anything for him to treat me the way he treated Joon. It never seemed fair.

"Is it wrong that I kind of want to see you do that?" I asked. "Does it make me a bad daughter, or a bad person?"

"No. It makes you human." He took my hand and laced our fingers together. "It takes more to be a parent than donating DNA. That man may be your biological father, but it doesn't make him a true parent. As much as I butt heads with Marauder, I don't doubt for a second if he'd known about me and Roe when we were kids that he'd have been there as much as he could. He's not the sort to shirk his responsibilities, and he's genuinely wanted a family."

"So I was just dealt a crappy hand? Is that what you're trying to say?" I asked.

"Something like that. But you know what? My family is your family. You gained a sister, a brother-in-law, and a dad. And I can promise any of them would go to hell and back for you because that's what you're supposed to do for your family." He tightened his hold on my hand. "In fact, the entire club would stand behind you. No one will ever mess with you again, Nari. If they do, I promise they'll regret it."

"It's going to take time for me to adjust to all this."

He leaned in to kiss my forehead. "Take all the time you need. I'm going to cut and season the chicken, then stick it back in the fridge until it's time to cook. Why don't you go relax for a bit?"

I nodded, knowing he wasn't trying to get rid of me. If anyone else had shooed me out of the way, I'd have thought I was being a nuisance. He'd already made it clear he liked being with me and spending time together. But I also realized couples needed time to themselves as well.

The idea of meeting the rest of his family terrified me, and yet, I also felt a thrill of excitement. Would I finally get to experience all the love and support Joon had all these years? It was like having one of my dreams come true, even if it wasn't going to be my own family showering me with love. Well, since I was married to Iron, they *were* my family now. I wasn't alone anymore, and I'd never would be again.

The thought filled me with warmth, and I couldn't help but smile a little.

Chapter Seven

Iron

I should have known Marauder wouldn't show up empty-handed, but this was a little much. "I thought I said to bring an extra chair. No one said anything about an entire set of furniture."

He shouldered past me, carrying one end of a table while Pyro had the other side. I saw six chairs in the driveway. What the fuck?

"You're married now. Don't you think you may need more than what you have right now? Consider this my *welcome to the family* present for your wife." He glanced around the living room. "Where is she?"

"Getting ready. She wanted to shower and change before you got here." Although, I'd told her she was fine just as she was, I could understand wanting to make a good impression. I also knew my family didn't give a shit. She could have greeted them in a shirt stained with grease and ripped jeans, and they would have welcomed her just the same.

Roe came in behind them and made herself comfortable on the couch and out of the way. Since my dad and brother-in-law seemed to have everything in hand, I decided to join her.

"Not going to help?" she asked.

"Nope. All I asked for was a chair." I shook my head. They really had gone overboard. "I'd told Nari she could decorate however she wanted. What if she hates that monstrosity?"

"Then Dad will understand." Roe leaned into me. "He's really excited. Try to go easy on him."

"Fine." I put my arm around her, and we watched as Pyro and our dad hauled the old table and chairs out of the house and finished setting up the new one. It was a good thing my kitchen had a large enough space for it. Technically, the area with the table was the breakfast nook. Or at least that's what Roe called it. Seemed awfully big for a "nook." Our dad's house had a formal dining room. At the moment, he didn't use it for much of anything, but now that Roe and I were both married, I had a feeling we'd be having family dinners and holidays at his place.

I heard soft steps coming down the hall and froze. Shit! I looked down at Roe's feet and realized I'd forgotten to remind all of them to take off their shoes.

"I hope she doesn't lose it," I muttered.

"What?"

"Go take off your shoes and quickly get Dad and Pyro to do the same," I said.

Her eyes went wide. "Oh no! I completely forgot you sent out a text about that."

Roe popped up and hurried over to the door. She toed off her flats, then chased after her husband and our dad to get them to do the same. By the time Nari reached the living room, everyone was barefoot or in socks. I tried to get a good look at the floors, wondering if she'd know. Had they tracked in dirt?

"You should have told me they were here," she said, her cheeks flushing. "I kept them waiting."

Roe came over and took her hand. "It's good to see you again, Nari. Is my brother treating you okay?"

"Better than I deserve," she mumbled. I lightly smacked her on the ass, then froze. She tensed and paled.

"Fuck. Nari, I'm sorry. It was an immediate reaction to what you said, but you know I wasn't trying to hurt you, right?" I asked. She gave me a quick nod, but the color hadn't returned to her face.

"What's going on?" Pyro asked.

"Nari was abused," Roe said softly. "And my brother is an idiot and forgot for a moment."

Nari looked up at me. "You forgot. So... You treated me the same way you would have even if I'd been normal?"

"You *are* normal. But yes, it's what I would have done in that situation regardless."

Our dad came closer, and he did his best to make himself appear smaller, although it was a lost cause. It was about the same as a tiger pretending to be a house cat. He gave her a smile and slowly held out his hands.

"Can I give my new daughter a hug?" he asked.

"D-Daughter?" she stammered.

He nodded. "You can call me Marauder or Dad. Whatever you're comfortable with. I didn't think my son would ever find someone who could put up with him. If he's ever too much for you to handle or you just need a break, you're welcome to come hide at my house."

She laughed a little and moved closer to him, letting him give her a hug. The look he gave me over her head told me how brokenhearted he was about the pain she'd felt from those who should have protected her. When it came to women and kids, he had a soft heart.

"You already met Roe," I said. "The other man is her husband, Pyro."

He cleared his throat. "We're all family. As long as the club isn't around, you can call me Cache."

My eyebrows shot up toward my hairline. What the fuck? I'd thought only my sister would ever be given that privilege. Nari already understood the significance, and it seemed to set her even more at ease.

"I'm still hoping you settle for calling me Dad."

Marauder finally released her and took a step back. "You have a present in the kitchen. If you don't like it, I'll take you shopping for a new one."

"That one *is* new," I pointed out.

"It's just money. What good is it if I can't use it to make my children happy?"

Well, fuck me. When he said shit like that, it made it difficult to get angry with him. I was still sore over the fact I'd had a shit life without a dad and a mother who didn't give a fuck about me. Then he'd go and say something like that, and I'd remember how excited he'd been when he found out he had two kids. Yeah, I was an asshole. At least I could admit it.

He took her to the kitchen to show her the table and chairs. We'd finished making lunch right before Nari took her shower, and I'd placed everything in the oven to keep it warm. Might as well eat while we were in here. I took down plates and carried them over to the new table.

"Do you like it?" I asked.

"It's beautiful," she said. "Actually, since it's black, I think I'd like to also paint the cabinets black, and maybe make the walls a light gray or maybe a blue or green. Would that be okay?"

"Of course. We can get some paint samples sometime soon. We'll roll some on the walls and you can decide which one you like best." I leaned to kiss the top of her head, then went back for the silverware and glasses.

By the time everyone sat down to eat, Nari had settled in and seemed to be enjoying herself. She smiled and chatted with her new family, and I found myself watching her intently.

"So, when can I expect grandchildren?" my dad asked.

Nari immediately went silent and glanced my way. I should have warned them to stay off this topic. Damnit.

"Nari was stabbed after she ran away from home. There's no guarantee she can have children." I tapped the table. "And even if she could, it doesn't mean we'd necessarily want any."

My dad stared at the table. "All right. I shouldn't have said something. Please forgive me, Nari."

"Jack said you were happy when you found out you had children. I'd imagine you've been eager to become a grandfather. My home life wasn't the best. I don't remember my mother, and my dad gave me a lot of the scars covering my body. I'm not sure I'd be a good mom, and the thought of having children and being responsible for someone so helpless scares me. I can't even take care of myself."

I reached over and took her hand. "I'm not overly fond of the idea either. But maybe once Roe and Pyro have some kids, we'll change our minds. For now, I just want Nari to get the chance to adjust to living here."

"Your family… are they local?" Dad asked.

"Yes. I heard my stepsister is dating the mayor's son. Her name is Joon. My father adores her and gives her everything she wants." She toyed with her food. "She's part of the reason I left. Sometimes she'd ask him to hurt me, and he would, without any hesitation. All because his precious Joon wanted him to."

"Jesus," Pyro muttered. I heard him grunt and knew Roe must have kicked him.

"I'm probably overstepping, and if so, just tell me." Dad held Nari's gaze. "The two of you may decide you never want children, and that's entirely up to you. I think you should see a doctor so you'll know if it would even be possible. I'd hate for the two of you to try and have a baby only to find out later that you can't."

Nari nodded. "You're right. I'm not sure where to go, or when. The thought of going into town is a little scary. My family doesn't know I'm back."

"Then Iron and I can both go with you. We can even have one or two of our brothers stay nearby in case there's trouble. Only if you're okay with that." Dad gave her a soft smile. "I'd hate to see you upset over something you can't control. Not all women can have children, and there's nothing wrong with adopting if that's what you end up doing. Or it can just be the two of you indefinitely. None of us are going to press you to do something you aren't comfortable with. All right?"

"Thank you... Dad." She said the last bit so softly I wasn't sure anyone heard her, until I noticed my father looked a bit emotional. Yeah, he'd caught that one word, and I knew it hit him hard. He was finally getting the big family he'd always wanted.

"Now, let's eat. Then we can come up with a plan for getting Nari to the doctor's office," he said.

"Everything looks great." Roe dug into her food, humming in appreciation with every bite. "Which one of you cooked this?"

"The meal was Jack's idea, and he cooked the chicken. I only helped with the veggies," Nari said. "I've never had much of a chance to cook, unless it came out of a box. Money was always tight whenever I even had a place to stay. There were times I lived on the streets."

I reached over and took her hand. "You can experiment with recipes as much as you want. Or if you decide you don't like cooking, then don't do it. I have no problem making our meals. My skills are limited. In fact, I looked up the recipe for this not too long ago."

"Have him grill you a steak sometime," Roe said. "My brother is great at grilling. But then I think most men are."

"I'll have to remember that." Nari smiled at her. "This is the nicest family meal I've ever had. At home, everyone ignored me, or found fault with everything I did. It's my first time joining the conversation, or people even caring what I have to say."

"We'll have many more of them," Dad said. "And you're welcome at my house anytime you want."

The rest of the meal went well, and Roe helped me clean up while Nari got to know Dad and Pyro better. She was right, though. This had been one of our better family meals. She wasn't the only one with a dysfunctional family. Although, I could admit to being mostly responsible for the tension in ours. Not anymore. It was time to accept the fact my mother had kept me from my dad. Not once had she ever given me a hint as to who he was. If I needed to blame anyone, it was her.

"I'm sorry," I said to Roe. "For everything. I know I haven't made any of this easy on you and Dad. I've been holding a grudge when neither of you were at fault."

"It's not me you should apologize to," she said. "And you know it."

"Yeah. I'll talk to him. Maybe not right this second, but I'll get it done. I want Nari to have a happy life with the family she's always wanted. If I'm always storming out when Dad's around, or arguing with him, then it's going to put Nari in an awkward position. You saw how easily she accepted him. I can't take that away from her."

"She must be pretty tough. If I'd had to live like that, I'm not sure I'd have made it. Knowing my family hated me would have broken me. Not her. Instead, she ran off on her own and managed to survive. She was lucky to come here and find you."

I shook my head. "No, I'm the lucky one. Just give her some time. We're taking things slow, despite the fact we're married, and I think it's going to take a bit for her to welcome random visitors at the house. Even if they're family."

"Come on. We should do the family bonding thing over movies. I know Dad would love it, and I'm sure Nari would too."

She was right. It was exactly the sort of thing my new wife would enjoy, and it was probably something essential for all of us. Now that I was willing to give Dad more of a chance, we needed the opportunity to bond as well. We'd been brothers in the club a long time, and I knew he'd have my back if something bad happened. But it was different letting him in as a parent.

For Nari's sake, I needed to make changes. Maybe for my sake as well.

Chapter Eight

Nari

The past few days had been nice, if a bit stressful. I felt closer to Iron and his family. Every day, his dad came by, and either Roe or Pyro would drop in here and there as well. I could tell they were trying to make me feel welcome, and I appreciated it more than they could ever know. Until now, I hadn't known what it felt like to be part of a family.

"Are you sure about this?" Iron asked, placing his hand on my hip. "There's no rush."

"I can't hide here forever," I said. "Your dad and Roe made the appointment for me. It's better to know than keep wondering. Even if we aren't sure we'll ever want children, this will still impact our lives."

He nodded. "You're right. Birth control or no birth control."

I closed my eyes and leaned into him, knowing he'd made the joke to set me at ease. Although, knowing Iron, he could have been serious as well. If I couldn't have children, we didn't have to worry about an accidental pregnancy. And if I could... Well, I'd discuss it with the doctor once we had results.

"What if you decide you want a baby one day? Not one you adopted, but someone who shares your DNA?" I asked. Honestly, I'd asked him probably a dozen times since I'd first brought it up.

"Nari." The warning in his tone was enough to shut me up. Yes, he'd told me countless times he didn't care. It didn't stop me from wondering what would happen if he changed his mind later. People had gotten divorced over less. "All I need is you."

"Sorry. I can't help it."

"I know." He kissed my temple. "In time, you'll

learn to trust I mean what I say. It's not right for me to expect it right off, especially after everything you've been through. Now come on. I hear Dad's new SUV in the driveway."

"Did he really buy one because Roe is expecting? He seems really excited about having grandchildren."

"Yes, he did. Although, I think it's partially so he can take you and Roe places as well."

"I wish I could have met you sooner," I said.

He snorted. "You're barely old enough as it is. Too much sooner and you'd have been jailbait. Although, the club still would have helped if you'd asked them. When you ran away, you could have come here and told Titan you were in trouble. Hades Abyss helps women and kids in need all the time."

"I was a little scared of your club back then. I'd heard mixed things. Some whispered you were into illegal stuff, while others said you helped people. I didn't know what to believe."

"Guess we need to work on our image some more." He took my hand and led me outside. He'd been right about his dad arriving. Marauder waved to us from the driver's seat. I'd expected Iron to ride up front next to him, but he slid into the back seat with me.

"And how's our little chick doing this morning?" he asked.

"I'm a person, not a bird," I said.

"Yes, but you're tiny and cute, just like a baby chick."

I couldn't even be upset with him. I actually liked the fact he'd given me a pet name. No one ever had before. Iron held my hand as we rode through the compound and out the gates. It felt like my heart skipped a beat, and not in a good way. Going into town scared me. If we ran into my family, I had no idea what they'd say or how Iron would react. They didn't know I was here. Or at least, I didn't think they did.

The fact my dad had promised me to someone in marriage made me wonder if he'd been keeping tabs on me. The thought of him knowing everything I'd been through and refusing to help infuriated me. What kind of parent did that? Marauder had been kinder to me than anyone in my family. I wished I could have had someone like him in my life before now. Things may have turned out differently.

"Roe didn't want you to think she was overstepping, but when she set up your appointment, she told them a little of what you'd been through. She didn't want them to be shocked by all your scars."

"It's okay." Seeing the doctor wasn't the issue. Although, I might change my mind once I met them.

"I know you're worried about your family," Marauder said. "We won't let anything happen to you, Nari. You'll be safe with us. You know that, right?"

"I do. It doesn't stop me from feeling anxious, though. I haven't seen them in years, and I didn't exactly tell them I was coming back to this town." Should I tell them my concern over my father knowing where I was? Or had they already figured it out?

"We'll get your appointment out of the way, and then stop by the diner for something. I'm sure you'll be hungry by then. They have really good pie," Marauder said. "No offense, but you could use some extra pounds. I may buy you two slices."

I knew he meant it in a good way. He was only looking out for me, and he wasn't wrong. I was far too skinny. I'd known it for years, but I couldn't exactly help the fact I'd been starving for such a long time. It wasn't like I'd ever had a lot of weight on me. My family had allowed me the minimum amount of food. Although, it had been better than what I'd been able to eat since I left.

We parked outside the clinic, and I took a breath to steady my nerves. I had no idea what to expect of the visit. How could they tell if I'd be able to have a child?

I fumbled my way through the new patient paperwork, having to ask Iron for things like our address and how we were going to pay. Since I didn't have insurance, he had to give them his credit card. I felt awful when I heard the amount. Why did it have to cost so much? He'd already spent a ton of money on me.

The wait left me feeling antsy, and by the time they called my name, I was ready to forget the entire thing and go home. Instead, Iron prodded me to stand up and follow the nurse. I paused, wondering if he wanted to be part of the visit, then decided against it. Once they saw the marks on my body, I didn't want them giving him rude looks. Even if Roe had explained everything, it didn't mean they would believe her.

"Miss Kaizer, you'll need to undress and put on a gown."

"It's Mrs.," I said.

She blinked and pursed her lips. What the hell was her problem? After she left the room, I changed and climbed onto the table to wait for the doctor. A knock sounded at the door before he came in.

"Hello! My name is Dr. Jackson. I know you were scheduled to see Dr. Lilian Andrews, but she was called out for an emergency." I tensed and wondered if it was too late to leave. I glanced at the door behind the doctor, and he followed my gaze before making a low humming sound. "Would you like me to go get your husband?"

"Please," I murmured. The thought of being alone with a strange man, even if it was a doctor, made me anxious. Logically, I didn't think he'd do anything to me with so many people in the office within shouting distance. It didn't stop the fear that filled me, not after everything I'd been through. The fact I could trust Iron, and now Marauder and Pyro, was a miracle.

He gave a quick nod and hurried out, only to return a minute later with Iron in tow. He came in and took my hand, as we both listened to Dr. Jackson's explanation of what to expect from the visit. Throughout the exam, Iron never let go of me. Even when they took me to another room for an ultrasound.

I felt better having him with me, but I still wished the female doctor had been available. I wondered if I could see her the next time I needed to come in.

"Everything looks good from what I can see," Dr. Jackson said. "But there is definitely some scarring on your uterus. I'd like to get a better look, but it's going to require tests at another facility. Are you okay with that?"

"Yes. I just need an answer," I said. "I hate not knowing if it's possible to have children."

Dr. Jackson nodded. "We'll do our best to help you. Someone from our office will call you with a date and time for the next test, and we'll go from there. It was wonderful meeting you both, although I wish it was under better circumstances."

After he left, Iron helped me dress and we checked out at the front desk. Since the ultrasound hadn't been covered in the visit fee, he paid even more money and set up a payment plan for the balance. I wondered how I needed to go about getting health insurance. It wasn't something I'd ever had to deal with before. Something told me the future tests would cost far more, and I didn't know if he could even afford it.

I held Iron's hand tight as we walked down the sidewalk toward the diner. Marauder was a few steps ahead of us, trying to give us a little space. Even though Iron had said he was fine not having children, I wasn't sure if I was. I'd always thought I'd never want a family. With the way I'd grown up, I didn't know how to be a parent to someone. Now that it seemed like I didn't have a choice in the matter, it left me feeling a little hollow.

"We won't know anything for sure until you have more tests done," Iron said. "He said the ultrasound didn't give him a good enough view of the scarring. After the CT scan, we'll either have an answer or move on to the next thing, which I Googled... it's called a hysteroscopy."

"I feel defective. My father always made it clear a woman's job was to take care of the house and her family, which meant having children. Not being able to do that makes me feel like less of a woman."

Iron drew me to a stop and put his arms around me. "You aren't defective or anything less than perfect. Stop worrying so much, Nari."

"What if all this medical stuff ends up bankrupting you? That visit was so expensive. Even if I looked at getting some sort of insurance, I don't think it would cover those upcoming tests. Doesn't that sort of thing take time to become effective?"

"Hey. None of this is going to empty our bank account. Even if we did start to struggle, I know the club would step in and help us however they could. I have a steady paycheck from the strip club but if I need more money, I can pick up an extra job here and there. The Pres always needs help with something."

We continued down the sidewalk, and I realized Marauder was waiting for us at the entrance of the diner. He held the door open for me, and a server greeted us right away.

"Welcome! Sit anywhere you like. I'll bring menus over in just a moment." The woman smiled and looked a little harried. As I glanced around, I realized she seemed to be the only one helping customers.

Marauder chose a booth along the front window. I slid into the nearest side and Iron sat beside me. It didn't take the server long to bring over the menus and some silverware.

"Do you know what you want to drink, or would you like a minute?" she asked.

Both men ordered Dr. Pepper, and I asked for water. She rushed off, stopping at two tables on her way behind the counter. For someone covering the entire floor herself, she seemed to be doing a great job. I hoped whoever was paying for our meal would tip her well. Poor woman looked like she'd been run off her feet.

"Get anything you want," Marauder said. "Just make sure you save room for pie."

He must really love the pie at this place, since he'd brought it up several times. I'd noticed I couldn't eat a full meal, no matter how hungry I felt. Regardless of what I ordered, if he really wanted me to have dessert, I'd have to take leftovers home or waste food. After living on the street, throwing out perfectly good food bothered me.

"You're thinking heavy thoughts again," Iron said. "What's wrong? Nothing on the menu you want to try?"

"It's not that." I explained what worried me, and he shared a look with Marauder. "What?"

"There's a church in town that has a soup kitchen once a week, and they take in donations of clothing for those who are either down on their luck or have chosen to live on the streets. It occurred to me that's not enough," Iron said.

"You were wondering how I managed to survive, weren't you?" I asked.

"Yeah. The thought of you scrounging through a dumpster bothers me. Honestly, I don't give a shit about anyone else in this town except my family and my club. It's knowing you were in trouble with nowhere to go that makes me realize the town needs more things in place for runaway teens at the very least."

I shook my head. "All they would do is have the police haul us back home."

The bell over the door jingled and I noticed Marauder's eyes narrowed. I looked over my shoulder and froze. Joon was here, along with two of her best friends. I hadn't seen her in three years. Nothing seemed to have changed. She still wore expensive clothes, had her hair styled the exact same way, and her makeup was minimal yet perfect. Just like her. Well, if you didn't count her terrible personality.

If it hadn't been for the fact we were the only Korean family in town, I'd have wondered how he recognized her. With a population of fewer than eight thousand people, I only knew of two other Asian families, and both were Chinese. Then again, Joon had always been popular. It probably wasn't his first time seeing her. Everyone greeted her everywhere we went, back before I'd run away.

"Maybe she won't notice I'm here," I mumbled. I

wasn't ready for a confrontation with my family. Then again, while her friends were around, and other people were watching, she'd probably be on her best behavior.

"If she causes trouble, let us handle it," Marauder said.

His words set me at ease. With the two of them on my side, I knew Joon wouldn't be able to push me into a corner. If I were really lucky, she'd be too scared of them to even approach me. I could hope, at any rate.

Chapter Nine

Iron

I didn't like how scared Nari became the moment she saw her stepsister. If I could, I'd get up and run that little bitch out of the diner. Sooner or later, she'd have to face her fears. I only wished it had come after she felt more secure with her place in my life. No matter how many times I said I was in this for the long haul and there wouldn't be a divorce, I could tell she didn't necessarily believe me.

My dad watched the girl like a hawk. She passed our table and found a seat in the center of the room. Naturally. From what I'd learned of her, she craved attention. I also saw the second she realized Nari was beside me. Her eyes widened slightly and her lips parted right before I saw a flash of anger cross her face. She schooled her features and smiled, then excused herself from her friends.

"Nari? When did you come back to town?" Joon asked in a syrupy sweet voice that made me want to gag.

"Does it matter?" I asked. Under the table, I felt her grab my thigh. She held onto me like I was her lifeline, and I realized it was exactly how she saw me.

"I wasn't talking to you." Joon's nose wrinkled. "Why is my sister with dirty bikers anyway?"

"They aren't dirty," Nari said in a soft voice. "And what I do has nothing to do with you, Joon. Just pretend I'm not even here."

I doubted her sister caught the whispered *you should be good at that*, but I sure the fuck did. My dad did as well, judging from his expression. I'd never seen him so angry before, except for when it came to Roe. Any time my sister was upset or in trouble, my dad lost his shit. He looked to be a few seconds away from exploding out of the booth right now. Looked like he really did think of Nari as his daughter.

"I believe what my wife is trying to say is she'd like you to leave us the fuck alone," I said.

"Wife?" She stared at Nari, then me. "What's that supposed to mean? She's already engaged to someone else."

"Funny. First time Nari heard anything about her engagement was after we were married." All right, not the least bit true, but she didn't have to know that. "How can she be engaged to someone without knowing about it? Seems a bit odd to me."

"I'm telling Dad about this," Joon said. "You just wait. He'll make sure you divorce this guy and come home where you belong."

My dad cleared his throat and glowered at Joon. "I suggest you move the fuck along. You even think of doing anything to my daughter-in-law or my son, and I will make sure you and your family regret ever coming to this town. I think you've hurt her enough already, don't you?"

"I don't know what you're talking about! Nari is a cherished member of my family." Joon gave another fake smile. "We've missed her so much."

"Why? Couldn't find another punching bag?" I asked. "Was it difficult to admit things didn't go your way not because of your older sister, but because you're a rotten human being?"

Ah. There it was. Her true self. Her features contorted and she let out a shriek before trying to rake her nails across my face. I grabbed her wrist about the time my dad stood up. He towered over her, and she shrank away. Or tried to. I wasn't letting the little bitch go.

"You can either return to your table or leave. Don't speak to Nari again, or my son. Do I make myself clear? As for your threats, I'll be sure Titan hears about it. After all, Nari is now part of the Hades Abyss."

Joon paled, and I knew she'd just realized how badly she'd fucked up. Her dad wasn't going to be able to get her out of this one, but I had a feeling they'd try. And once the club knew trouble could be heading our way, they would rally around us, even if Nari hadn't been comfortable enough to meet everyone yet. Looked like our time had run out.

"Can we just go?" Nari asked. "I don't want to stay here with her."

My dad grunted and flagged down the server. "Can we get three slices of apple pie to go? I'm afraid your clientele has spoiled my daughter-in-law's appetite."

The woman eyed Joon. "This one?"

Marauder nodded. "We'll come back some other time."

The woman huffed. "No need. You, get the hell out of my diner."

Joon's jaw dropped. "Excuse me? You're making *me* leave?"

"Yes. My house, my rules. Now get out of here. You and your friends don't bring in nearly as much profit as their club does. The Hades Abyss are dedicated customers. If they refuse to eat here because of you, then I don't want you here."

Joon and her friends stormed out. I saw the other two girls had turned bright red. Clearly, their friend had caused a problem and they didn't want any part of it. I wondered how much longer they'd keep speaking to Joon.

"Sorry about that," the server -- who apparently was also the owner -- said. "I just bought this place last month. I have enough trouble keeping the diner staffed. I can't have some spoiled little girl running off my best customers. The pie is on the house today."

She hustled off, checking on her other customers along the way. Nari leaned into me. I put my arm around her, cuddling her close as my dad retook his seat. He stared at the owner of the diner with a thoughtful expression. It seemed I wasn't the only one taken by surprise.

"She's amazing," Nari whispered. "She owns this place and she made Joon leave."

Marauder smiled a little. "I think our Nari has a case of hero worship. Better watch it, boy, she might decide she likes that woman more than she likes you."

"Shut it, old man."

Nari's cheeks flushed. "I won't ever like anyone more than Iron. But I do wish I had half her confidence. I want to be bold and assertive like that one day."

"If that's really what you want, then we'll help you get there," I said. "For the record, I adore you just the way you are. Don't feel like you need to change for anyone other than yourself. I'll support you no matter what."

"Even if I decided to get ten piercings, cover myself in tattoos, and shave my head?" she asked.

My dad nearly hurt himself, he laughed so hard. I couldn't believe she'd even come up with something like that. "Yeah, even then. Although, I may cry over the loss of your hair. I know it wasn't healthy when you first got here, and it will take some time, but I know it's going to be beautiful."

Her cheeks turned even pinker. "I wasn't really

going to do all that."

"I know." I kissed her cheek. "Although, I think some tattoos might be sexy on you. And maybe a nose piercing."

She covered her face and shook her head. "I don't see me volunteering for pain any time soon. Or ever."

True enough. Some people needed that shot of pain to cope with everything in their lives. Whether or not she got anything pierced or inked was entirely up to her. I didn't care either way. As long as I had her, that's all that mattered.

The bell jingled again and Joon stepped inside with an older Korean man. Nari's father, I presumed, as well as a police officer. Now what?

"Can I help you?" the owner asked.

"Nora, I hear there's some trouble. This girl says she was threatened by your customers, then you tossed her out," the officer said.

Marauder stood and I held up a hand to stop him. Instead, I slid out of the booth and approached them. If things went sideways, I wanted him to get Nari out of here.

"Officer, I think there's been a misunderstanding," I said. "That girl came over to our table to harass my wife. My dad and I decided we'd just leave instead of dealing with her."

"And I reserved my right to refuse service to anyone I choose and told her to leave. The Hades Abyss are my best customers," Nora said. "Besides, if I were them, I'd be filing assault charges against the girl. She tried to claw this one's face off."

The officer sighed and looked up at the ceiling. I saw the muscle in his jaw tick, and I realized Joon had left out a few things when she went running to her daddy. Maybe the town didn't adore her as much as Nari thought.

"Officer, what Nora said is true. Joon said some stuff I took as a threat to my wife, when I told her she needed to go back to her table or leave, she tried to rake her nails down my face. I caught her wrist before she could make contact." I looked at Nari's father. Yeah. The word "wife" hadn't made him the least bit happy.

"Nari is engaged to someone. A man of good standing in the community," he said.

"Well, I'm afraid you'll have to cancel the engagement she knew nothing about since we're already married." I leaned in closer and lowered my voice. "But if you'd like to discuss it alone, I'd be more than happy. I'd like to have a few words with you about the way you treat your daughter. I bet she could sue your ass for assault and emotional damage. Or don't you want everyone to know you beat her until she was scarred from the neck down?"

The officer pinched the bridge of his nose. "Mr. Kwon, I think you haven't been completely honest with me about the situation. This sounds more like a family dispute. As far as the diner, Nora is right. She can ask anyone to leave if she doesn't want to serve them. I suggest you settle this amongst yourselves."

"Oh, I'd be delighted to," I said. I'd settle, all right. I wanted nothing more than to put that fucker in about a dozen graves, because I was going to tear him apart.

"I didn't hear that," the officer muttered before walking out of the diner. It seems he understood me just fine. Nari's dad, on the other hand... the glare he gave me said he thought he still had control of Nari. I'd show him just how wrong he was.

"Mr. Kwon, I'd suggest you and your family stay the fuck away from my wife. We're not getting a divorce. She's not returning to your home. And she sure the hell isn't marrying anyone else. You're more than welcome to push the issue, and I'll be overjoyed to put you in your fucking place. As for the little bitch next to you, I'd prefer to never see her again. If she so much as breathes in my direction, I may decide to teach her a lesson. You know, like the ones you've given Nari most of her life."

He straightened and tipped his chin up. Yeah, the fucker understood me loud and clear. We'd see if he was smart enough to heed my words.

Mr. Kwon left with Joon, and Nora heaved a sigh.

"Sorry about that," she said. "Those two think they own this town, especially since the girl is dating the mayor's son. They've been trouble for a while now."

"None of this is your fault. In fact, my wife thinks you're amazing for standing up to them."

"So, she's the other daughter?" Nora asked. "I wondered. Used to see her around town, then one day she vanished. Word on the street was that she went to stay with relatives or go to some fancy boarding school. Guess that wasn't true, huh?"

"Not even a little. She ran away from home because her father was beating her. I'd appreciate it if you could keep an eye on her if you see her around town. Because of those two, she's scared to leave the compound."

"Don't blame her one bit. Those two are evil far as I'm concerned." Nora clapped her hands together. "Now. I'm honored you'd ask me to watch over her, but I think she could use a little pick-me-up right today. You already asked for pie. Does she like milkshakes?"

"I haven't seen her drink one yet. Let me ask."

I went back to the table and sat beside Nari again. "Nora wants to know if you like milkshakes."

"I do, but they make me sick."

"Probably shouldn't drink it, then," I said. "Anything else you want? I think she wants to give you something special for having to face those two monsters."

"Technically, I only spoke to Joon." She smiled. "But I like hearing someone call them monsters."

Nora came over. "What's the verdict?"

"Milkshakes make her sick," I said.

"Well, that's a shame. Whatever meal you order is on me for today, honey. And I promise this will be a safe space for you from now on. Those two aren't allowed in my diner ever again." Nora placed her hands on her hips. "So what's it to be? Any idea what you're craving? My cook makes amazing chicken and dumplings."

"That sounds good," Nari said. My dad and I ordered burgers and fries, and Nora went to place our order with the cook. The way Nari watched her gave me an idea.

"From the talks we've had, it seems like you feel you don't have anything you're good at, or a way to contribute. Nora appears to need some help. Would you want to try working here part time? Maybe a few hours a week to see if you like it?" I asked. Of course, I had no idea if Nora would actually hire her, but she might.

"I might enjoy that," she said. "Especially if I got to work with Nora. Maybe her bravery would rub off on me."

Nora returned with our drinks, which I hadn't even realized were missing until now. Too much had happened since we entered the diner.

"I heard your conversation," she said. "If you want to help me out, I'd sure appreciate it. You could try serving coffee and wrapping silverware to start. Then work your way up to waiting on customers at tables. We can discuss pay and hours if you decide you want to work here."

"I'll be happy to bring you and stay for the first few times," my dad said. "If Nora doesn't mind me taking up a spot at the bar or one of her tables."

"Not at all," Nora said.

The way Nari lit up, I knew this was the right thing for her. And as long as someone from the club made sure she got here safely and back home, then I didn't have an issue with it. However, I wanted to deal with the Kwons as soon as possible.

Nora pulled out a pad from her apron and wrote something on it. When she placed it on the table, I saw it was her name and two numbers.

"The top one is the diner number, and the bottom is my cell phone. You can call either one anytime you want. Let me know if you decide to try working here. And even if this is too much for you and you just want a woman to talk to, I'd be happy to take your call. You seem like a sweetheart compared to that rotten sister of yours."

"Stepsister," I corrected. "We appreciate it, Nora."

"Food will out in a few minutes."

She left us alone as she went about her business, and Nari kept staring at the paper with the numbers on it. I folded it and stuck it in my wallet.

"I'll give it to you when we get home. That way

you won't lose it between here and the house," I said.

"I meant what I said, little chick. I have no problem coming here with you a few days to see if this is something you want to do. As long as the Pres doesn't have a job lined up for me, then I'm free to do whatever I want," Dad said.

"Thank you. Both of you." She took a deep breath and let it out. "I think I'm ready to meet the club. I can't very well try to come into town to work at a job if I can't even handle being around the men in your club, right?"

I nodded. "I'll text Titan now and let him know."

Nari is ready. Set up a family night.

It only took him a moment to respond. *On it.*

I had a feeling we'd either get an alert today or tomorrow about a family dinner at the clubhouse. I only hoped Nari was ready for this. Either way, I'd make sure someone always kept an eye on her when she left the compound. I wasn't taking any chances with her safety.

Chapter Ten

Nari

I'd changed my clothes several times. Even with all the new things Iron had bought for me, nothing seemed like the right outfit for meeting the rest of his club. I wanted them to like me. The screen-printed tees were cute and comfortable, but I thought they might make me look childish, especially since I was so flat-chested.

"Stop worrying so much," Iron said. "You're my wife. Titan already knows everything, and so does the VP. Even if it's your first-time meeting everyone, you're already a part of the Hades Abyss."

"I can't help it. I'm not used to being accepted so easily, or anyone actually wanting me around."

"I know." He leaned down and kissed me softly. We hadn't shared a passionate kiss yet. For once, I wondered if I might be ready. "You're beautiful, smart, and sweet. What's not to love, Nari?"

"You make it sound like you love me."

He remained quiet and stared at me. The fact he didn't deny it made me feel… I wasn't sure I could put it into words. Both thrilled and scared? Was there a single word for that type of emotion? Even though I didn't really remember my mother, I was certain she'd loved me. There was a vague memory of being happy before her death. No one had since then. The thought of Iron being in love with me… it was a little overwhelming.

"Have you ever thought about that word?" Iron asked. "Love. There are two types. The first is a deep affection for someone. Right now, I feel that one a lot when it comes to you. The other is the passionate type of love. That one tends to be driven more by sexual desire, and while I sure the hell want you in that way, I think my love for you falls more under the first definition."

For some reason, I thought it was better that way. If you loved someone only because you desired them, wouldn't that type of love eventually fade or go away completely? But a deep affection? That sounded like something long-lasting.

"If that's what the word means, then I love you too. I can't imagine my life without you. Well, I can because I've been there, and it was a cold, dark, miserable existence. I may be unsure of myself rather frequently, but I've never felt more secure or happy in my life."

He hugged me tight. "I'm glad you feel that way with me. Now come on. It's time to meet everyone else. Dad, Roe, and Pyro will all be there."

He led me out to the new SUV we'd found in our driveway one morning. No one would admit to knowing how it got there. Iron said since it was already registered in our names, it was most likely Wizard who had done it. The hacker wasn't saying anything, though. I hadn't driven it yet. The thought of getting behind the wheel terrified me. I hadn't driven a car in three years.

When we reached the clubhouse, I saw a line of vehicles as well as a crap ton of motorcycles. I wondered how many of them had other transportation. Iron had also said the club had a few trucks they used for hauling stuff and odd jobs. I remembered seeing one of them the day he'd taken me to his house. A Prospect had driven it to deliver my things.

The moment we pushed the doors open, everyone in the clubhouse went silent. I didn't like having so many people stare at me. Iron clasped my hand and led me farther into the large room. A bar ran along one wall, and the opposite side had tables and chairs. Someone had set up two long tables and filled them with food. I saw coolers underneath.

"Everyone, as I'm sure the Pres told you, I have a wife now. This is Nari. She's a little skittish, so go slow and don't mob her," Iron said in a loud voice.

Two women came forward, smiling widely. I'd noticed one had been standing next to the club president. They both looked close to the same age.

"I'm Delilah, and I'm with Titan," she said. "Welcome to the Hades Abyss. I know they can be a bit loud and sometimes scary. It will take some time for you to adjust, but I promise you're in good hands."

"And I'm Phoebe," the other one said. "Titan's daughter."

I looked from her to Delilah and back again. "Um..."

They both broke into laughter. Delilah pointed across the room to some children. "That little boy is mine. His name is Walker. I'm actually younger than Phoebe."

"The other two with Walker are mine. Banner and Ember. I already had them when my dad met Delilah." Phoebe looked over to a man standing near Titan. "And that's Kraken. He's mine."

The doors opened behind us, and a tall redheaded man stepped in with a tiny woman next to him. Well, compared to him anyway. She still was taller than me. She gave me a little wave.

"Sorry we're late. I'm MaryAnne. This is Patriot."

"It's nice to meet... everyone," I said.

Iron tugged me over to a table and sat, then pulled me down onto his lap. I hadn't seen Marauder, Roe, or Pyro but they magically appeared and took the other seats. With familiar faces surrounding me, I felt a bit better. I hadn't realized how tense I was until just then.

"I'll get you some food." Marauder stood again. "What do you want, Nari? There's fried chicken, sandwiches, burgers, pulled pork barbeque, beans, chips, and quite a few desserts."

"I'm not sure I could eat much right now," I said. "Maybe a sandwich?"

Iron lightly tapped my hip, letting me know that wasn't enough. He was always pushing me to eat more food. If I hadn't known it came from a good place, I might have been angry with him.

"I'll bring a little of everything and you eat whatever you want," Marauder said. "Once you have a few bites, you may realize you're hungrier than you thought."

"Your family…" MaryAnne stopped and bit her lip. "Um, are you related to Joon Kwon?"

"She's my stepsister." I really hoped the two of them weren't friends. I didn't think it was possible, considering what Joon thought about the men in this club, but stranger things had happened.

"She's mean," MaryAnne said. "No offense."

Iron snorted. Yeah, calling Joon mean didn't begin to cover it. It was almost too nice a word for her.

"I prefer referring to her as a little bitch," Iron said.

"She's part of the reason my father hurt me so much," I said. "She'd tell him I did something like steal her boyfriend, and she'd beg him to punish me. He'd end up nearly beating me to death. And no, I didn't take her boyfriend from her. I didn't want anything to do with him, but if anyone she liked so much as spoke to me in passing, then she'd lose it."

"You're going to make them all pay, right?" MaryAnne asked, directing her question to Iron.

"Oh, yeah. I'm going to make sure the Kwons can't ever hurt her again." Iron kissed the back of my shoulder. I didn't know what he planned to do to them, and I didn't really care. As long as I didn't have to deal with them again, that's all that mattered to me. But I secretly hoped he hurt them as much as they'd hurt me.

Another man walked over, keeping a few feet between us. "I'm Wizard. I know you were listening when I spoke to Iron on the phone before. Thought you might need to put a face with a name."

"Thank you for all the help you've given me," I said. "You didn't have to do all that."

"Yeah, I did. And there are some things we need to discuss. I did more digging on that issue of your surprise engagement. I'll follow the two of you home after this and give you all the details about the deal your dad made with Michael Sanders."

"This is going to piss me off, isn't it?" Iron said.

"Since I'd like to kill the man with my bare hands, and I'm *not* married to his daughter, yeah. You're going to want to tear his head off." Wizard backed up a step. "I'll let someone else have a chance to speak with you. Don't worry, Nari. Nothing bad is going to happen to you."

The rest of the club came by one at a time to introduce themselves. I even got a chance to meet the children. I felt more at ease with them than the adults. Although, watching how gentle everyone was with the little ones was enough to make me feel safe with them.

I ate a little of everything Marauder brought to me, including a piece and a half of pie. By the time I pushed the plates away, I felt so full I thought Iron might have to roll me out the door. Iron tapped my thigh and I stood. With a quick kiss on my cheek, he walked off toward the bar. I wasn't sure what to do at first, then I noticed Marauder and Pyro were going to join him. Roe remained at the table, and MaryAnne came over to join us.

"What's it like living with Iron?" MaryAnne asked. "He seems so cold. Even Patriot said the guy is kind of a jerk."

"Really? He warned me people would say something like that, but I haven't seen that side of him. With me, he's always sweet and protective."

Roe snickered. "I'm the only other person who's experienced what a nice Iron is like. And even with me, he can still be prickly at times. He's completely different with you, Nari, which is a good thing."

"Don't even get me started on different." MaryAnne pointed at Roe. "Do you have any idea what kind of man you married? He was a complete psycho before he fell for you."

"I'm assuming all their names mean something," I said.

"Patriot is ex-military, and probably the most patriotic person here," MaryAnne said.

"Kraken was in the Navy," Phoebe said, coming over to join us. She pulled up a chair, and Delilah took the last empty spot at the table. "I'm going to go with my dad being so tall and big. If it's for any other reason, I really don't want to know."

Delilah's shoulders shook with silent laughter. I had a feeling she thought Titan's name was given to him for another reason, and I was right there with Phoebe and not wanting to know for sure.

"Pyro got his name because he tends to set things on fire," Roe said.

"Do I even want to ask how Marauder got his?" I asked.

"Probably not. None of us have been brave enough," Phoebe said. "If Kraken says that man is crazy and not to piss him off, then I'm going to give him a wide berth if he looks mad. Something tells me if anyone tries to hurt you, Marauder is going to be one step ahead of Iron and doing some damage."

"What about Iron?" MaryAnne asked. "Has he told you how he got his name?"

I shook my head. I hadn't even thought to ask. The fact he let me call him Jack, and no one else was allowed to, had been enough for me. While I might be a little curious about the name Iron, it wasn't enough for me to go digging for information on him. If he wanted me to know, he'd tell me.

"Do you like living here so far?" Phoebe asked.

"I think so. I have to admit I haven't really ventured out of the house until yesterday. Going to the diner was nice, until Joon showed up. Nora, the woman who owns it, was really sweet. She said I could try working there part-time to see if I liked it."

"Are you going to give it a try?" Delilah asked.

"I'm not sure. It could be fun, and I'd like to earn some money and feel like I'm not relying on Iron for everything, but the thought of my family catching me away from the compound is rather scary."

"So, wait until Iron and Marauder have that situation sorted out," Phoebe said. "Or you could ask Titan to assign a few guys to keep an eye on you when you venture out."

Roe cleared her throat. "No offense, Phoebe, but that didn't work so well for me. I think she needs to stay behind the fence as much as possible. If they could kidnap her or hurt her in some way, then it sounds too dangerous to me."

"I heard you were kidnapped," I said. "And it happened while the club was watching over you?"

My heart started to race, and I suddenly wanted to go home and hide under the covers. If my father got his hands on me, I knew it wouldn't end well. I didn't even have to hear about the plans he'd made with Michael Sanders.

"The men following me and Phoebe got separated from us at a traffic light. By the time they caught up to us, the man who kidnapped me had already snatched me and run. He'd knocked Phoebe out and left her in the parking lot." Roe tipped her head toward Jacob and two children. "That's when I met Jacob. He kept me safe and decided to prospect for the club afterward."

"I met him before. He's big and a little scary, but seemed nice," I said.

"He is." Roe smiled. "That man has a heart of gold. Even when he protected me, he wouldn't hurt anyone. Not even the evil people. He doesn't have a mean bone in his body."

"Which makes him an odd fit for this place," MaryAnne said. "My Patriot is the sweetest man ever. To me. The people who hurt me? He didn't hold back. I know he'd kill someone if it meant I would be safe and not feel scared or threatened."

"In case you were wondering, my brother will be like that with you," Roe said. "I have no idea what he's planned for your family, but I can promise he won't let them off easy. Your father may end up disappearing."

It should bother me, hearing that my husband could take a life so easily. Maybe if I thought he was killing someone innocent it would be different. My father was a rotten bastard. I wanted to be the one to hit him. He'd used a belt and cane on me so many times. The thought of making him suffer the same fate lit a fire inside me.

"Hmm. I know that look," Phoebe said. "Make sure you tell Iron and Marauder you want a piece of your father when they get their hands on him. Otherwise, there won't be anything left when they're done. I get it. Being able to fight back when you know that bastard can't retaliate? Nothing sweeter."

"We've all had hard lives before coming here," MaryAnne said. She rubbed her hands up and down her arms. "I was locked up in a place where I should have been treated well. Instead, the guards abused me. Raped me. And the doctors were in on it. Men terrified me until I met Patriot."

"The man I'd thought was my father sold me to another club," Phoebe said. "A preacher, no less. I never knew Titan was my father. I'd already been here, living with Kraken, when we found out. The other club offered me up to him, hoping to sweeten whatever deal they had going. When Kraken saw Ember, and realized what they'd done to me, he wanted to burn the place to the ground."

Delilah shrugged her shoulder. "I don't have a horror story. My dad was overprotective and my brothers were just as bad. So I left town, came here, and became a web cam girl. Or so I thought."

Phoebe laughed. "Yeah, turns out the only one watching her was my dad. He'd fallen for her right away, even if he couldn't admit it."

"So you aren't alone," Roe said. "All of us are here for you, and so are the guys. You have a new family now. One who will cherish you, love you, and accept you exactly as you are. All right, my sweet sister?"

I nodded, feeling warm inside at her words. "All right."

MaryAnne reached over to take my hand. "I hope we get to know each other better. I'd like to be friends."

"Same here," Phoebe said.

"Me too." Delilah smiled. "I heard Titan scared you that first night. He won't hurt you, even if he yells. Think of him as a grumpy teddy bear."

"Only she can call him that," Phoebe said.

"If you need anything, want to talk or hang out, you call one of us or all of us. We'll help however we can." Roe stood up. "But for now, I think I want my husband to take me home. I'm getting kicked to death."

I eyed her stomach and wondered what it felt like to be pregnant. The thought of bringing children into this world scared the shit out of me and yet, I was a little awestruck by the fact she had a life growing inside her. I wondered if I'd ever get to experience that. Now that I felt more at ease around these people and like I was making some friends, the idea of starting a family didn't seem quite as far-fetched as it had before. If I had everyone here to help me watch over them, then having children might not be so bad.

I glanced over at Iron and watched him laugh and talk with the other men in the club. He'd said he'd never thought about being a father. I had a feeling he'd be good at it. If the tests came back saying I couldn't carry a baby to term, then I'd take it as a sign I wasn't meant to be a mother. But if I *could* have children... well, I might need to discuss it with Iron again.

Chapter Eleven

Iron

I handed Wizard a beer, then sat next to Nari at our new kitchen table. It was time to find out what the hell her father had been up to. Then I'd decide just how painful I'd make his death. One way or another, I was ending his life. He'd done so much damage to my sweet wife and didn't have even the slightest bit of remorse over it. Men like him didn't deserve to keep breathing.

"What did you find?" I asked.

"What do either of you know about Michael Sanders?" Wizard asked.

"Nothing," Nari said. "Only that he's one of my father's business partners."

"And are you aware of the type of business your father does?"

She shook her head. Why was I getting a bad feeling about this? Wizard was tiptoeing around the issue, which meant it was bad. Really fucking bad. "Just spit it out and stop stalling."

"Your father owns what's pretty much a sweatshop. Not here in town. It's a warehouse in the same area where those assholes took Roe. He's bringing women and children over from Korea, promising them a brighter future, then literally working them to death," Wizard said.

"And this Sanders person is helping?" I asked.

"He helps manage the place. He also has a thing for Asian women." Wizard cleared his throat. "Um, not sure how to say this without freaking out Nari. There's video footage of him coercing the women into having sex. If they still refuse, then…"

"He rapes them," I said. Wizard nodded.

Motherfucker! And Nari's father wanted her to marry someone like that? What the fuck was he thinking? No, clearly he didn't give a shit about her, or anyone else. I couldn't understand how he could do something so horrific to women and children.

"Can we help them?" Nari asked softly. "Those women and children? Is there a way to get them out of there?"

"We can, and we will," Wizard said. "Might need some help, but I promise we won't leave them there."

"What about Nari's engagement to Sanders?" I asked. "Why would he do something like that?"

"From what I've been able to find, it looks like Nari's stepmother had the idea for the business. She lured her new husband to America, convinced him this was the best way to earn money, and there was only one pesky issue she needed to deal with. Nari."

I leaned back in my chair. "Because she's Kwon's actual daughter?"

"Yeah. Even if Kwon wrote Nari out of his will, she could contest it. It doesn't look like stepmommy-dearest wants to share anything with Nari. If she marries her off to Sanders, the man will keep Nari in check."

"What about Joon?" Nari asked. "Does she know about any of this?"

"Yes. In fact, she's visited the warehouse a few times. I found camera footage of her. She's even nastier than Sanders. The things I saw... I'll spare you the details. You won't be able to eat for days."

"What the fuck?" What was so awful it even turned Wizard's stomach?

He leaned in to whisper so Nari wouldn't hear. "Kwon keeps the kids there until they're fourteen.

Then they disappear. Joon enjoys forcing the thirteen- and fourteen-year-old boys to make her come, but only after she's humiliated them and literally whipped them into submission."

Joon was a year younger than Nari, which meant she was eighteen. How the fuck could she be so twisted already to do something like that? It made me realize she'd known exactly what Kwon had been doing to Nari and probably enjoyed every second of it. Crazy fucking bitch! I hoped the devil had reserved a special place in hell for her, because I'd be sending her his way soon enough.

"What's going on?" Nari asked. "What did Joon do?"

"I'm not telling you. It's really bad, Nari. She abuses the children." Hopefully that would be enough to satisfy her curiosity and she'd leave it alone.

"I don't like the idea of them being there," she said.

"I know, sweetheart. We'll save them. I promise." I reached over and took her hand. "Wizard, why does Sanders want Nari other than her being Asian?"

"As long as neither he nor Nari try to claim money from the Kwons when Mr. Kwon dies, then they'll get to keep fifty percent of the business, and Mrs. Kwon guarantees fresh employees every year for as long as the business is operational and Sanders is married to Nari. Otherwise, he'd have to fight it out in court, which... There really isn't a way for him to do that without the law seeing what sort of place they're running. He'd be screwed out of millions of dollars." Wizard tapped the table with a finger. "And that's the most puzzling part of all, or was. I couldn't figure out what the hell they would make there to earn so much cash. Until I started tracking the male children after they were considered to be no longer useful."

"What happened to them?" I asked.

"Underground fighting. There's a ring one state over. The boys are sold to that place, forced to fight, which is often to the death, and are never seen or heard from again. Boys in good health go for ten thousand each."

"How does that come out to millions?" I asked.

"That's the really twisted part. Rich women who want mixed race children pay a stud fee. When the boys are sixteen and seventeen, they not only have to fight, but if they're proven breeders, then Kwon gets another fifty grand per kid. Took me a while to find it, but not all the boys he brings over go to the warehouse. Some are already fifteen, and he sells them straight to the fighting rings."

"How many?" Nari asked.

"Three per month at first and now he's up to five or six per month," Wizard said. "Mortality is high in that place, so they go through a lot of kids. He's bribed someone not only in Korea and immigration here in the US, but a few other countries as well. Sanders isn't the only one who gets off on forcing himself on women. Kwon whores out the women and girls, and sometimes the boys, to make sure his business runs smoothly."

"I think I'm going to be sick," Nari muttered.

She wasn't the only one. Looked like I'd need to make Sanders disappear too. Four people in a town this size? Especially with one of them dating the mayor's son... this wasn't going to be easy.

"I know what you're thinking," Wizard said. "I'll help you however I can, even if it's laying false trails for them leaving the country. It's been done before. I'm sure we can make it work."

"It's going to take time to plan. I'm not sure we have as much as we thought," I said. "Not if we're going to get those people out of there."

"What about the ones in the fight ring?" Nari asked.

"Not something we can handle." Wizard leaned forward and braced his arms on the table. "I'm not saying we're going to leave them to their fates. I can make some calls, with Titan's permission, and see if some other clubs are willing to step in and clean up that mess."

"Are all the boys Asian?" Nari asked. "My father can't be their only supplier."

"He's not, and yes, they are. Japanese, Chinese, Korean, and Filipino. There may be more, but that's what I was able to track. Why do you ask?"

She licked her lips. "Yakuza. If they have Japanese boys, the Yakuza may step in to handle it. They'll most likely recruit them, but it's better than where they are now, isn't it?"

"And the others? I'm not sure the Yakuza would let them live," Wizard said.

"The Jo-Pok could get the Korean boys out. I'm not sure if there are any in this country. Is there a way to reach them and find out?" she asked.

"Is that like the Yakuza?" he asked.

"Yes. For the Chinese boys, you'd need to contact the Triad. Unless they're the ones who sold them. This is going to be too much for you, isn't it?" Nari asked.

"Probably, but I know other hackers. If they aren't busy, I can get their help following the trails. Know anything about the Philippines?"

"They have Yakuza there, and quite a few gangs. I'm not sure who would be best to extract the Filipino boys." Nari slumped in her chair. "How could my father do such a thing?"

"Did you find anything on her dad before they moved here?" I asked.

Wizard gave me a sharp look, and I knew he wasn't going to say anything in front of Nari. Which meant I needed to get her out of the room. *Shit.* There wasn't a way to do this without it seeming suspicious.

"I actually have some club business to talk about before I go," Wizard said.

"Nari, I need you to step out of the room. That's the one thing you can't be part of. If anyone says the words 'club business' it means you need to make yourself scarce."

She stood and placed her hand on my shoulder. "I'll go wait for you in the bedroom. There's a show I wanted to watch, so I'll be entertained while you're talking."

I lifted her hand and kissed her fingers. "I'll make it quick if at all possible."

Once I heard the bedroom door shut, I eyed Wizard. Did he really have club business or was he just giving me an easy way to make Nari leave? He lifted his finger over his lips as a sign for me to remain quiet. I strained to listen for something, then heard the TV start in the bedroom.

"Had to make sure she wouldn't hear us," he said. "In case you didn't figure it out, I lied. Nari really doesn't need to hear this, though."

"So what was her dad up to before coming to this country?"

"When she said Jo-Pok, it jarred my memory. I'd seen that somewhere and didn't place it until a minute ago. Her mother was the daughter of someone pretty high up in organized crime in Korea, and her dad was your typical thug. I'm not sure why the two got married, but I think he may have killed his wife when their marriage didn't gain him any traction over there."

"What do you know about the stepmom?" I asked.

"She was a prostitute in Korea. Joon's father is listed as someone who died before she was born. It's possible he really was her sperm donor, but I don't think so. I have a feeling she got knocked up and panicked. There are a few years where I couldn't find anything on her. When she popped back up, it looks like she was on the fringes of stuff Kwon was into. I don't have proof, so don't say anything to Nari."

"You think they conspired against her mom," I said. Wizard nodded. It fit what we knew about them so far. The entire family was fucked-up, except my wife. How the hell did I get an angel from that horde of demons?

"So what do we do now?" I asked.

"For now? Nothing. I'm going to talk to Titan, then reach out to the other hackers. Once we have a game plan in place to rescue the women and kids at the warehouse, you can do whatever you want to the others. I'm guessing you'll want a piece of Sanders too."

"Oh, yeah. That fucker is mine. When I think of the things he'd probably do to Nari, I want to tear out his throat."

"She's yours, Iron. No one is taking her from you. I made sure it looked legit. There's no way for them to file for divorce on her behalf."

"What if they paid someone to make it happen?" I asked.

"Hmm. Good point. When I get home, I'll find a way to create a bank error that will tie up their funds for at least a few days. It's the best I can do for now without making them aware something is up."

"I appreciate it."

Wizard finished his beer and put the bottle in the trash. "I'll keep you in the loop as we move forward. Just take care of Nari until then."

"Now *that* I can do without any hardship." I smiled. "She's pretty amazing, isn't she?"

"One of a kind." He shook his head. "All of you go ass over teakettle when you find the one, don't you?"

"Just wait. Your time will come."

Pain flashed in his eyes for a brief moment before he smiled again. "Nah. I think I'm a confirmed bachelor."

I got the feeling there was a story there, one no one knew. Clearly, we didn't know as much about Wizard as we thought. If he wanted to keep something personal a secret, I wouldn't stop him, no matter how curious I felt. Had he already loved someone and lost them? Or was it more of an unrequited thing?

I locked up behind him and went to the bedroom, where I found Nari stretched out on her stomach watching TV. Her feet were crossed at the ankles and she had her chin resting in her hand.

"Is it good?" I asked.

She gave a little yelp and stared at me with wide eyes. "You scared the crap out of me! When did you get in here?"

"Just now." I ran my hand down her thigh. "Is that what you're into? Those pretty boys?"

She narrowed her eyes at me. "Obviously not, because I'm married to a surly biker everyone calls cold. Although he sounds a little jealous right now."

I nearly smiled. It looked like she'd finally

figured out her place in my life. Meeting the club had brought her out of her shell a little more, and the discussion with Wizard had been good for her as well, even if she'd heard some awful things. I hadn't seen her quite as animated. Once she'd relaxed at the clubhouse, she'd opened up to the ladies and had a good time.

"You're so beautiful," I murmured. We hadn't had sex yet, even though Bones had called with the all-clear a few days ago. She'd brought it up once, and I'd backed off, knowing she wasn't ready. But now... I thought maybe she was.

Dropping to my knees beside the bed, I kissed her thigh right above the bend of her knee. Her breath caught as I placed another kiss a little higher. She didn't stop me, and the tension in her body felt different from before. This wasn't a fear response. No, my pretty little wife was getting turned on.

"Jack, can we... I mean, are you going to stop and push me away again?" she asked.

"No. If you say you're ready, then I'll believe you. God knows I want you."

She rolled onto her back and held her hands out to me. I lifted myself onto the bed, caging her. My gaze held hers, looking for even the slightest bit of hesitation. When I didn't find any, I lowered my head and gave her the kiss she'd been waiting for. My lips teased hers before I flicked my tongue against the seam, asking for entry. She opened and let me in.

I devoured her, not giving her a chance to catch her breath. Every fucking night I'd dreamed of this. She'd been my wife for a week. Now I'd make her mine in every way possible. I'd show her what it meant to be my wife, to be loved by someone like me... I only hoped she could handle it.

Chapter Twelve

Nari

My heart fluttered and I felt a little dizzy. No one had ever kissed me like this before, and if I'd been standing I knew my knees would have given out. Even as he dominated me, I felt secure with Iron. No matter what he did, I knew he'd never hurt me. Even now, if I told him I was scared, he'd stop and leave the room.

But I didn't want him to. I felt ready and I knew we needed this. I didn't know how he'd been so patient with me. I tugged at his cut, wanting him to take it off. Iron pulled away and shrugged out of the leather, then set it aside. He grabbed the back of his collar and pulled his shirt over his head. I took it from him and tossed it aside.

With a wink, he stood and unfastened his belt. I watched every move as he undressed. Heat pooled inside me, and I squeezed my thighs together. It was the first time I'd desired a man, and I couldn't wait for what would happen next. The others hadn't cared if I enjoyed myself. All Iron had to do was touch me and I went up in flames.

"You sure, Nari?" he asked.

I nodded and sat up on my knees so I could undress. He'd already seen me naked several times. I wasn't sure what to do. Did he want me to lie down again? Should I offer to suck his cock? He'd liked it when I got him off in the shower, but that was all I knew of my husband as far as sex went.

"Lie back and put your hands over your head," he said. "And if I do anything you don't like or something that scares you, say something and I'll stop. You have all the power right now, Nari. Understood?"

"I know, Jack. I trust you."

I stretched out and placed my hands over my head like he'd said. He grabbed my legs just above my knees and dragged me to the edge of the bed. Bending my knees toward my chest, he then spread me open. The hunger in his gaze made me want him even more. I'd never felt as beautiful or sexy as I did right now.

He ran a finger over my pussy lips. "I never asked, but do you trim this?"

I knew why he'd asked. While I did have hair there, it wasn't a lot. "No. It's always been like that."

"I like it." He parted the lips and leaned in, dragging his tongue over me. When the tip flicked my clit, my thighs tensed and I nearly saw stars. I'd never realized how sensitive I was right there, since none of the men I'd been with seemed to care I even had a clit. "You still doing okay?"

His tongue flicked against it again, and I bit back a moan. "Less talking, more licking."

He chuckled and proved to me he'd only been playing until then. He brought me close to orgasm multiple times but always backed off at the last second. I felt frustrated, but it also made things more intense.

When Iron sucked my clit into his mouth, I came, screaming out his name. He continued to lick and tease me until I'd come twice more.

"Tonight is all about you," he said.

"It's still too early to be considered night."

Iron winked at me. "I'm only getting started."

Oh, God! I had a feeling I wasn't going to be able to walk by tomorrow. He stood and picked me up, readjusting me how he wanted. Iron stretched out beside me, his hand sneaking between my thighs. He swirled two fingers over my clit before sliding them inside me. As he pumped them in and out, he used his thumb to rub the hard little bud.

I still had my arms over my head, and he leaned in to lick and nip at my breasts. His teeth grazed my nipple and my hips bucked as pleasure shot through me.

"Looks like I found a sensitive spot," he murmured before doing it again. Between the wicked things he was doing with his mouth and his fingers driving me mad, I wasn't sure I'd stay sane for much longer. The man was making me crazy.

I lost track of how many orgasms I had. Everything was so new it was like I was a virgin. When he flipped me onto my stomach and yanked my hips into the air, I gripped the sheets. Iron rubbed his cock against my pussy, bumping my clit with it. After the fourth time, he eased inside me. I felt the burn as he stretched me. I'd never been with someone his size before. While he wasn't overly large, most of the men who'd taken me had dicks that weren't bigger than three or four inches when fully erect. Iron had to be at least six inches.

"You're thinking too much, which means I'm doing something wrong." He hauled me up so my back pressed to his chest. "I'm going to get you all worked up, then you're going to ride my cock until we both come."

"Please, Iron! I want that. Want it so much."

He smacked my hip. "I don't want to hear that name on your lips when I'm balls-deep inside you. Who am I, Nari?"

"Jack."

"That's right." He pinched one of my nipples while his other hand teased my clit. It wasn't long before I couldn't sit still. At first, my movements were a little jerky and uncoordinated, but I was soon bouncing on his cock. When I came, I felt the gush of my release. "Fuck, yeah! You have no idea how hot it is you came that hard."

He nipped the side of my neck then kissed my shoulder. I couldn't stop. The feelings coursing through me were addictive and I wanted more. I don't know how he held back, but I came another three times before he wrapped an arm around my waist and put me back on my hands and knees.

Iron took me hard and deep, driving into me like he'd become possessed. His grunts and groans turned me on even more. He slid his hand down between my legs again, and one brush of his fingers was enough to make me come one last time. I heard him muttering.

"Fuck, yes! Feels so damn good. Fucking perfection."

Even after I felt the heat of his cum filling me, he kept thrusting into me. He finally stopped, his breathing ragged and his skin sweaty. Iron kissed my back, then pulled out. Our mingled release ran down my thighs.

"Need to clean up," I murmured.

"Not yet. Let me hold you a few minutes, then we'll go shower."

"Is it supposed to be like this? Because it never has been."

His hold on me tightened. "Only when you find the right person. This was a first for me too. Love you, Nari. You and only you."

"Love you too, Jack."

He held me hostage in his arms, and I heard a soft snore from him a moment later. He dozed for at least twenty minutes before I knew I needed to use the bathroom. I struggled to get free and finally managed. After I relieved my bladder, I started the shower. It must have awakened Iron, because he came up behind me, placing a hand on my waist.

"You could have slept more," I said.

"Showering with you sounds much more fun."

Why did I get the feeling he didn't plan to *only* shower? I couldn't say I was upset about it. Even if I was sore tomorrow, it would be worth it. Being with him was amazing and made me feel normal... wanted. Actually, I felt so many things I couldn't label them all.

I stepped into the shower and under the spray. He joined me, closing the door behind us. Placing my hands on his chest, I felt the steady *thump* of his heart.

"You sure you're okay?" he asked.

"Positive. Just a little overwhelmed, but in a good way."

"Remember, you're in charge. Tell me to stop or ask for more. I'm yours to command."

I smiled and leaned forward, kissing the center of his chest. "You shouldn't say things like that. The power of you being mine to control may go to my head. What if I ordered you to kill everyone who ever hurt me?"

He stared down at me, his eyes going dark. "Already have plans for your family. You give me names and last known locations, and I'm happy to take care of the others."

"You do realize you just agreed to murder people for me, right?"

His eyebrows arched. "And your point? Nari, I told you I'm not a nice man. Won't be the first time I'm covered in blood."

His words should have scared me. If he'd even once raised his voice at me or lifted a hand to me in anger, I might have been. My father was a monster, yet everyone thought he was an upstanding man. Well, most everyone. It was men like my father I needed to fear. Guys like Iron might appear rough, but no one had been sweeter to me than he had. So no, the thought of him killing the people who'd hurt me wasn't the least bit terrifying.

"Punishing the wicked doesn't make you a bad man, Jack. It makes you a hero."

"I can definitely say no one has called me that before." He cupped my cheek. "Makes it even more special that my wife thinks of me that way. Pretty sure you're the only one, though."

"Aren't I the only one who matters?" *Holy crap. I didn't just say that, did I?*

My heart thumped in my chest, and I realized I felt braver around him than anyone else. Never before would I have dared to say such a thing. The way he smiled told me enough.

"You're so fucking cute sometimes. I'm glad I'm the one who saw you with Titan that first night," he said. "Otherwise, some other lucky bastard would be standing here with you."

I shook my head. "I don't think I'd have trusted anyone else."

I wasn't just saying the words either. I meant them. Whatever it was about Iron, he'd put me at ease from the beginning. Intrigued me unlike any man had before. Somehow, I knew we were meant to be together, even when I doubted my ability to remain by his side. The longer we were together, the more I could picture a life with him. Not only this week or next month, but even further than that.

"When you say things like that, it makes me want you even more. I want to leave a mark on you, show the world you're mine." He grinned. "Guess that makes me a possessive asshole, huh?"

"A little. But I like it." Belonging to Iron felt

incredible. No one had wanted me before him. With Iron, I got to experience so many new things... including what it felt like to be cherished.

"Our first shower, you took me by surprise," he said. "Do I get to play this time?"

I nodded, not trusting myself to voice the words. I couldn't think of anything I wanted more right this moment.

He pulled me closer and lowered his head, devouring my lips. I clung to him, not sure my legs would hold me up. It was almost as if he could read my mind when he lifted me. I felt the tile against my back and hooked my legs around his hips. His cock brushed against me, and a shiver raced through me.

Drawing back, he held my gaze as he slowly sank into me. His cock stretched me wide, and I whimpered at the sting of pain. Yeah, it would hurt tomorrow, but I didn't care. At least this was a pain that came with pleasure.

"Who are you, Nari?" he asked, his voice low and rough.

"Your wife."

"That's right. You're mine. *Only* mine. Anyone who tries to take you from me will pay the price."

He pinned me to the wall as he took me fast and hard. I couldn't catch my breath as my nails dug into his shoulders and it felt like every nerve in my body lit up. Iron hit just the right spot inside me, and I came so hard I nearly saw stars. He kept thrusting, claiming me, branding himself on my soul, until I felt the heat of his release.

"Think you can go again?" he asked.

"Maybe in a bit?" I winced as he eased out of me and put me back on my feet. Yeah, that was going to hurt for a day or two. "Or not."

Wait. How the hell was he able to go again so soon? Most men I'd known couldn't get it up for at least an hour, and Iron was older than them. I wasn't about to ask, though. The last thing I wanted to do was offend him.

He smirked. "Sorry."

"You don't look it," I mumbled.

He chuckled and leaned down to kiss me softly. "I am sorry it hurts, but no... I don't regret doing that. In fact, I'd do it all night long if I thought you could handle it."

"I think I'd need to work up to that." Assuming it was something that could be done. Maybe it was our size difference and it would always hurt after one or two times. To me, he was more than blessed in that department, although most would probably call him average.

"Let me wash you, then we can head to bed. I'm sure you're tired."

"A little," I admitted. Was he going to hold me? I'd never known I liked to cuddle until Iron.

His touch was gentle as he cleaned me. After I rinsed, he nudged me out of the shower. I dried off and watched him through the glass. The brisk strokes he used to bathe himself made me wince. If he'd scrubbed me like that, I might have felt like he was taking off a layer of skin.

I dressed in my nightgown and a pair of panties, then climbed into bed to wait for him. Staring up at the ceiling, I couldn't help but wonder about my family. Both my father and Joon had been run out of the diner. Even the officer hadn't seemed inclined to side with them after hearing the story. To them, image was everything. Would they retaliate? Or would they actually be afraid of the Hades Abyss?

"You're thinking awfully hard," Iron said, rubbing a towel over his hair. He tossed it into the bathroom and got into bed beside me, pulling me into his arms.

"Worried what my family will do next," I said.

"Doesn't matter. They can't hurt you anymore, Nari. Want me to prove it?"

"How?" I asked.

He picked up his phone and called someone. After he put the call on speaker, he showed me the screen. *Wizard.*

"If you're calling to give me more work, I'm hanging up," Wizard said the moment the call connected.

"You're on speaker with Nari in the room. She's concerned her family will do something after being tossed out of the diner earlier. Help me reassure her they aren't going to be a problem."

"Um." Wizard cleared his throat. "You sure you want her to know everything?"

"He already offered to kill anyone who's ever hurt me," I said. "Is it worse?"

"Nope. That about sums it up," Wizard said. "In that case, we've managed to put trackers on every vehicle your family owns. In addition, I'm using the cameras around town, as well as the home security system at the Kwon residence to monitor their every move. They won't be able to do anything without me knowing about it."

"Thanks, Wizard. If something happens, let me know. I want this wrapped up as soon as possible," Iron said. "My wife can't relax as long as those people are running loose."

"Not a problem. For now, I'll keep an eye on them, and I'm working on a few other surprises."

"Like what?" I asked.

"You've mentioned their reputation means everything to them. I'm just going to put a few cracks in it. Enough for people to question the type of family they really are. Should be enough to break up Joon and her fiancé as well."

"Thank you," I said. "Is it wrong I want them to suffer as much as I have all these years?"

"Not at all. Revenge can be the sweetest thing ever," Wizard said. "Let us do the dirty work, but, Nari, if you want to see them one last time, tell Iron. Otherwise, it'll be too late."

The call ended and I sighed. I should have felt horrible, like an evil person for wishing them all dead. But after learning how awful they truly were, I couldn't help but think getting rid of them would make the world a better place. I wasn't the only one they'd wronged.

"The other hackers are working on getting those women and kids to safety," Iron said. "Once we know your family won't be able to make them disappear, then we'll make a move. Just give us a little time."

"I may stay behind the gate until then, if that's all right. I feel like I'd be tempting fate to walk around in the open."

He nodded. "If that's what you want. I'll call the doctor tomorrow and see if he can schedule your next test for a few weeks from now. I'll just tell him something came up we need to take care of first."

"Thank you, Jack. For everything."

"You're my wife, Nari. My family. Besides, if I didn't do at least this much, I'm pretty sure my dad would kick my ass. He seems to really like you."

I smiled and snuggled into him. He was right. My own father might hate me, but Marauder had decided I was one of his own. His little chick. Even though I'd been to hell and back, I'd finally found the place where I belonged.

Chapter Thirteen

Iron

The time had finally come. I'd been waiting on Church to be called all fucking day! Actually, I'd been waiting for a week. Wizard had wanted to make sure he had enough data to give everyone for this to go smoothly. But things were finally looking up. It seemed as if everything had fallen into place overnight. Nari wanted revenge, and she would have it by nightfall. Even if I didn't know everything going on, Titan wouldn't have called all of us here if it wasn't time to make our move. I'd left Nari at home with Roe and Titan's kids. They'd stopped by just as I was leaving, which made me wonder if Roe had simply wanted to keep Nari company, or if Pyro had told her to go to my house.

Titan banged his fist on the table to get everyone's attention. "As you all know, Iron is married now, and his woman arrived with trouble following her. Nothing we haven't faced before. Wizard has prepared some information for all of us. I'm going to let him take the floor for a bit."

Wizard stood and passed folders to everyone around the table. "That's the bare bones of what we're up against right now. Nari's family is seriously twisted, including her younger stepsister. The goal is to capture the Kwons and take them to a secure location."

Someone let out a whistle as they flipped through the files, and I heard a few others mumbling to themselves. It wasn't the first time the Hades Abyss had taken on something like that. I didn't know if this particular chapter had, but the Missouri chapter I'd only left this year had taken out the trash plenty of times.

"I'm assuming they won't be leaving in one piece," Stone said.

"We're going to let Iron and Marauder have them," Wizard said. "And I think Nari wants a chance to say her final piece."

"What's the deal with the workers?" Galahad asked. "It says we don't have to worry about them. Did you call another club to get them out? Won't people find it odd this place vanished so fast?"

"Wire and Lavender offered to make the closing look legit and less suspicious. Any funds will be put aside. If Nari wants them, she can have them. Otherwise, they will be used to help women and children in need. As for another club helping... Not exactly." Wizard tossed more papers into the center of the table. "Turns out Nari's mother was well-connected. As in, her family is part of one of the largest crime organizations in Korea, the Jo-Pok. No idea why Kwon thought it was okay to fuck with them. From what we've pieced together, he likely married Nari's mom as a way to advance his rank in the organization. It didn't work. While I don't have definitive proof, I did make a convincing enough argument that Kwon killed his wife."

"You contacted her family?" Gatsby asked.

"I did. The Yakuza are going to handle anyone who would have fallen under their jurisdiction. It looks like Kwon was stealing kids out from under their noses with the help of a corrupt, lower-ranking member. Something tells me he's already dead, and if I hadn't guaranteed Kwon's death, they would have stolen him from us to make him pay for his transgressions." Wizard sighed. "I can't guarantee they won't groom the boys they save and turn them into Yakuza. Either way, they'll have a fighting chance and go back to their home countries."

"So other organizations are handling the kids. What about the women?" Galahad asked.

"We have two clubs getting them out," Wizard said. "Our only focus is on the Kwons. I've been tracking their every move, and they'll be easy to snatch. But we're going to have to send three teams to handle it."

"What about the asshole she's engaged to?" I asked.

"That one is a special case," Wizard said. "There's someone else who would like to deal with him. When I sent out the call for help, one of the clubs recognized him. The bastard raped and tortured a woman before killing her. Bad news for him is that woman was the baby sister of a club VP. As much as I know you'd like to get your hands on him, I offered him up to them instead."

I nodded, understanding why he'd done it. In fact, I knew whoever the VP was, he would torture the fucker more than I would. He had a debt to settle, and Sanders was going to be begging for someone to end his suffering. Of that I had no doubt, because it's exactly what I was going to do to the Kwons.

"Where are we taking them?" Menace asked.

"The shed."

Enough said. Everyone here knew where he meant. Getting Nari there would be interesting. I didn't want her to stay and see exactly what we did to her family, but she needed time to tell them to fuck off in her own way. I'd have to see if a Prospect could take her there and bring her home. Dad and I wouldn't be leaving until those pieces of shit were dead.

"Any volunteers for the teams?" Titan asked. "Boomer and I are hanging back. Wizard will also be here to keep an eye on the cameras around town, make sure we can pull this off smoothly."

"I'll go," Menace said. "Never condoned hurting women, but I'll help capture Joon. That girl has earned her spot in hell."

"I'll take Mr. Kwon," Stone said.

"I'll work with Menace." Galahad shoved the file away from him. "Sick bitch deserves whatever she gets."

Patriot lifted a hand and Titan shook his head. "Not you. I understand why you want in on this, but I need you here to help keep an eye on the women. Especially MaryAnne. She'll worry the entire time you're gone."

"Something I don't know?" I whispered to Stone, who was sitting next to me.

"Their daughter, Blaze, is sick. MaryAnne panics if anything happens to that girl. She's their only kid," Stone whispered back.

"Fine." Patriot sighed. "I feel fucking useless, but I get it."

"You know what your woman is like," Titan said. "She's gotten stronger than when she first came here, but if anything happened and you were injured, she'd lose her shit."

"I know," Patriot said.

"I'll go with Stone," Gatsby said.

"Any volunteers for snatching Mrs. Kwon?" Boomer asked.

Smoke and Poison both raised their hands. I hoped two men each would be enough. None of the Kwons seemed like the fighting type. I doubted any of them stood a chance against my brothers, but I'd have felt better if we had more men assigned to each one.

"I'll text each group the location of the Kwon

they need to grab, and I'll alert you to any changes. I'm sure you'll want to discuss the best possible way to get them with as little fuss as possible." Wizard pulled out another stack of folders. "These are all the details on each of them, including their schedules and any deviations over the last several days. It should help you narrow down the best time and place to complete your mission."

"What is this, a video game? Mission? Seriously?" Galahad snorted.

"Call it whatever you want," Wizard said.

"Iron and Marauder will be ready and waiting. Once all three Kwons are at the shed, they'll meet you there. Any idea how you're going to handle Nari?" Titan asked.

"I'd like a Prospect or another brother to drive her over. She doesn't need to see what happens once she's gone," I said.

"I'll do it," Bones said. "I think she'll be comfortable enough to ride in the truck with me."

"Thanks," I said. He was right. Nari should know by now she could trust him. The others... she might need time to not feel so anxious around them. Logically, she knew she was safe with anyone at this table. Emotionally, she was still damaged and traumatized from her past. It would take time for her to heal all the way.

"Then Church is dismissed," Titan said. "Just keep me up to date on what's going on."

I stood and made my way outside to my bike, only to find my dad already waiting for me. Since we'd need to respond when we got the text the Kwons were waiting for us, we'd already decided ahead of time to stick together. Which meant he was heading home with me to spend time with Nari. I'd told her not to overdo it, but I had a feeling she'd made lunch for us. Sandwiches would have been fine. It wasn't like we were picky. Nari kept saying she felt like a bad wife because she didn't really know how to cook, so I'd gotten her a cookbook and she'd tried something new every day.

"Wonder what's on the menu for lunch," Dad said. "What was it she made for dinner last night?"

"Um. I think she said it was some sort of squash pasta." Whatever it had been, it was fucking fantastic. At this rate, I was going to gain a shit ton of weight if I didn't start working out again.

"I'll meet you there," Dad said. "I have a feeling this may take a while."

I nodded, knowing he was right. Each group would need to plan their attack to minimize the risk of getting caught. It would most likely be tonight, if it happened today at all. I did think it was best to snatch them at the same time, or as close to it as possible. If one went missing, the other two would be on alert. But none of it was my call.

Dad pulled into the driveway next to me when we reached the house. Nari opened the side door and waved at us. The scent coming from the kitchen made my mouth water. Walking into the room and seeing the food already on the table was certainly a surprise. I also noticed Roe wasn't anywhere to be seen.

"Did my sister already go home?" I asked.

"She and the kids left about ten minutes ago. Pyro texted when Church was wrapping up, and she wanted to hurry home and figure out what to feed everyone. I offered to make enough for all of us, but she looked a little queasy while I was making our food." She folded her arms over her chest. "Exactly why were Titan's kids with her today, anyway?"

"They slept over last night," Dad said. "Banner really likes Roe, and Phoebe looked like she could use a break. Roe offered to let them camp out in the living room."

"Well, I guess it was good practice for her." Nari shook her head. "Those kids are a bit exhausting, though. I don't think they slowed down for two seconds."

"What did you make? It smells incredible."

"Pork belly with spicy rice cakes. I decided to try making Korean food today. If you don't like it, there are hot dogs in the fridge as a backup."

I kissed her temple. "I'm sure it's amazing. Can't wait to try it."

My dad nodded as he took a seat at the table. "Never really had Korean food. I've ordered Chinese takeout, but this looks different. Smells better."

"You know, if Dad likes this stuff, he'll be over here all the time asking you to make it for him," I said.

"I'm okay with that." Nari smiled. It was good to see her so happy.

I had to admit, her food was incredible. The way my dad ate everything on his plate and looked around for seconds told me we'd be seeing him rather often. Then again, he already stopped by frequently. Nari seemed comfortable with him, and I could tell he loved her. She finally had the support she'd needed all these years. If only I'd been able to meet her a little sooner. The thought of all she'd suffered ate at me.

"You know I still want some names," I said. "And I'm sure Dad does too. Why won't you let us rid of you all your nightmares?"

"Taking care of my family is enough. The others aren't even worth mentioning. None were as bad as my dad," she said.

"If you ever change your mind, you just let us know," Dad said.

* * *

Nari

They hadn't said anything, but I could tell they were going to keep me in the dark as much as possible. Iron hadn't made it a secret they were going to capture my family. I also knew he planned to kill them. So why wasn't he telling me what was happening? I'd asked to confront them one last time. Would he actually let me?

It had been a waiting game all day, and now it was nearly dinner. I wasn't sure about starting anything if it meant we'd have to leave before it was finished cooking. My stomach grumbled at me, and I knew I'd have to figure something out soon. I might have been starving most of my life, but after living with Iron and getting three meals a day, my body now expected to be fed at regular intervals.

"Would it be okay to order pizzas for dinner?" I asked. "We could invite Roe and Pyro over."

Iron and Marauder shared a look before my husband nodded. I saw him pull out his phone and I assumed he was texting his sister. Marauder took his out as well, tapped on the screen a few times, then handed it to me. He'd opened a pizza app and I stared, not quite sure what he wanted me to do.

"Um. What am I ordering?" I asked.

"Get whatever you want," Marauder said.

"But I don't know what everyone else will want." He simply stared at me and pointed at the phone in my hand. I'd learned enough about him to know he wanted me to order something I felt like eating. After I selected a thin crust supreme, I handed the phone back. It took him a few minutes of adding things before the order must have been complete because he put his phone away.

"Did you tell whoever is on the gate to watch for an order?" Iron asked.

"No. Didn't think about it," Marauder said.

"I'll handle it." Iron sent another text, then handed me the TV remote. "Why don't you find us a movie to watch?"

I gripped the plastic controller in my hand. Why did they keep asking me to make decisions about things? Sure, dinner and a movie might not be a huge deal, but it still stressed me out. I always worried I'd choose something everyone hated. Part of me knew they wouldn't complain or care. The other part was still stuck in the past where one wrong move would end with me being in pain for days.

I found a comedy and quickly put the remote down. It wasn't very long before the front door opened and I saw Roe and Pyro come in. They removed their shoes and joined us in the living room. Iron had already had to add a shoe rack to the mat by the front door to have enough room for the entire family's shoes. The men's boots went on top, and my shoes and Roe's went on the bottom shelf. Still not ideal, but it would work for now. I'd have preferred an enclosed porch where everyone could leave their shoes, but I wasn't about to ask Iron to build something like that.

"Everyone okay in here?" Pyro asked. "Still no news?"

"Nothing yet." Iron reached over to take my hand. "Food should be here soon."

Roe sat on the other side of me. "How do you feel right now?"

"I'm not sure. Ready for everything to be over. Does that sound awful? I mean, I've condoned killing my family. What sort of person does that make me?" I asked.

"The kind who's tired of taking their shit," Pyro said. "No one here blames you for wanting them gone, Nari. In fact, every brother in this club is ready to tear them apart. We've got your back, okay?"

I nodded. His words made me feel a little better. I knew murder was wrong, but so were all the awful things my family had done not only to me but other people as well. I didn't think they'd shared all the details yet, but from what I'd gleaned, my family was into some really bad stuff. I'd take horror movie monsters over them any day.

"I'm the good girl out of everyone at the Hades Abyss," Roe said. "For what it's worth, I don't have a problem with your family being punished. If we'd handed everything over to the law, they'd have gotten some prison time and eventually been released, or possibly been deported. I'm not really sure how all that works. What I do know is the Hades Abyss is going to make sure they can't hurt anyone ever again."

Her words calmed me. "Thanks, Roe."

She gave me a one-armed hug. "That's what sisters are for. Put those awful people in your past. You have a real family now."

She was right. Iron hadn't just given me a safe haven, or his love… he'd given me everything I'd ever wanted or needed. Now I just had to face this one last hurdle and then I could move on.

Chapter Fourteen
Iron

It took two days for my brothers to round up the Kwons. When the text came in, I was more than ready to get vengeance for everything they'd done to Nari. While I was pissed about their trafficking and abuse of women and children, the abuse my wife suffered weighed heavier on me. Probably because she was mine. It had taken them time to coordinate their efforts and snatch the Kwons without anyone noticing.

"Nari, are you sure you want to go?" I asked, giving her a chance to back out. As much as I loved that she wanted to face her fears, I also worried seeing them again could cause a setback in her recovery.

"I need to do this," she said.

"Fine. Bones is going to drive you over in a club truck. Once you've asked your questions, yelled, or done whatever you plan to do, then I'll have him bring you home."

She narrowed her eyes at me. "Why am I being sent home?"

"I don't want you to see that side of me. It's not going to be pretty. We're going to make them feel as much pain as possible before we kill them." I ran a hand down my face. "Telling you about it, and having you witness it firsthand, are two different things. The last thing I want is for you to become scared of me when you realize what I'm capable of doing."

"Jack, everyone is capable of violence in the right situation. Most choose not to do it. Doesn't mean they can't. And who said you get to make them suffer? Why can't I get some vengeance of my own?" she asked.

"Are you serious right now?" I'd thought she'd want to talk to them, or tell them to fuck off. Not once had I considered the fact she might want to hurt them physically by herself. If it's what she wanted, then I wouldn't get in the way. I only hoped it wouldn't haunt her later.

"Very much so."

"All right. Then you need to do this the right way. You're not dressed properly." I folded my arms over my chest and waited while she rushed off to the bedroom. At least she'd known what I meant, or I hoped she did. Nari returned a few minutes later in jeans, the boots I'd bought for her, a black tee, and her new property cut. I didn't know how Titan managed to get it made so fast, but I'd given it to her last night.

"Better?" she asked.

"Yeah. Now you look like a biker's wife."

She wrinkled her nose. "At least you didn't call me an old lady. I know it's just a term and doesn't mean I'm literally old, but I really don't like it. I much prefer being called your wife."

"Some of the guys don't want to get married. Doesn't stop them from claiming someone. In that case, they can't be called a wife."

"Fine. I see your point. Can we go now?" she asked.

I wondered if I should be concerned that she seemed too eager. Exactly what did my pint-sized wife have planned for her family? I glanced at my dad, and he gave me a subtle shake of his head. Looked like he didn't know either. Why did I get the feeling I might regret this later?

"Bones is here," Dad said.

"Nari, we're going to head out first and Bones will follow. Take your time when we get there. You don't have to race inside right away. Gather your thoughts and prepare yourself for whatever hateful things they may say."

"It doesn't matter anymore," she said. "They can't hurt me now, and you've shown me what it means to truly be part of a family."

She hurried out to the truck while Dad and I got on our bikes. Bones backed down the driveway, then waited for us to take the lead. The shed was in a remote place on the Hades Abyss property. Far enough away from any other homes or businesses, no matter what happened inside no one would hear us. Of course, Titan had also soundproofed the place as much as he could.

Menace and Stone were both standing guard when we arrived. I gave them each a nod as I got off my bike and went inside. Dad was right behind me.

"You won't get away with this," Mr. Kwon said.

"Why not? You've been getting away with all kinds of things for over a decade. Murdering your wife. Trafficking women and children. Beating your daughter and selling her off to a monster. Should I continue?" I asked.

His expression sobered. Ah. Looked like he hadn't realized we knew so much about him. Good. I hoped he realized exactly how bad his situation was right now. The two women glared at me and remained silent. Then it was like a mask slid over Joon's face. She smiled, gave me an innocent, wide-eyed look, and even batted her eyes a little.

"Whatever you think I've done, I promise it wasn't me," she said. "I'll even be willing to make it worth your while if you untie me. I'm sure I can please you better than Nari."

Disgusting. I couldn't stand the little bitch. "Sorry. I'm too old for you."

The smile slid off her face. "I'm younger than

Nari by only a year. How does that make you too old for me and not for her?"

"Don't you like your men on the more illegal side? You know, like fourteen- and fifteen-year-olds?"

My words hit their mark and she paled. Her gaze dropped to the floor, and she finally realized we had shit on her too. Mrs. Kwon didn't even bother trying to weasel her way out of anything. Made me wonder if we'd missed something in all our digging. She'd been the only one to remain silent. Did she have more to hide than the other two?

The door opened behind me, and Nari came in. Her father immediately started yelling at her in rapid-fire Korean. Nari stopped beside me and tipped her head to the side, staring at him like a confused puppy.

"Sorry, Father. You made sure I don't remember how to speak Korean. I have no idea what you're saying," she said.

"How could you betray your family?" he asked, his voice hard and ice cold.

"Family? I'm sorry. Since when do families beat and starve their daughters? Do they sell them off to monstrous men who rape and kill women? I don't think so. You're not my family. None of you are, and never have been. You made sure of that."

"Nari, are you responsible for this?" Joon asked.

"Mmm. Yes and no."

"Which is it?" Mr. Kwon asked.

"Well, you're technically here because of me. You see, my husband didn't like hearing all the things you've done to me over the years, or why you did them. I'm guessing the reason is Joon and the step-bitch from hell. Oops. I mean stepmom." She smiled at him. "So he decided you needed to be taught a lesson. All of you. Or rather, once he discovered all your crimes, as well as those of the women in the family, he decided to just wipe you out entirely."

Mrs. Kwon glowered but remained silent. Joon snarled and yanked at the ropes binding her to the chair. Only Mr. Kwon dangled from a hook in the ceiling. His toes barely scraped the ground. Wouldn't be long before his shoulders ached, if they didn't already.

"Did anyone get his cane?" Nari asked.

"Yeah. Think it's in the truck," Menace said. I hadn't realized he'd come inside. "I'll get it for you."

He returned quickly and handed the cane to Nari. She approached her father with determined steps. The look in her eyes took me by surprise. I'd never seen her so cold or vicious before. Without even hesitating, she drew back the hand holding the cane, then slammed it against Kwon's ribs. He gave a bark of pain and grimaced.

"You can't even take this as well as I did," Nari said. "I learned early to remain quiet. Don't you remember? Crying or screaming only made the beating worse. Guess I should teach you the same lesson."

We stood back and watched as Nari took all her pain, fear, and frustrations out on her father. She hit him with the cane as hard as she could, repeatedly. The skin over his ribs and knees broke. The way some of his joints were turning black and blue made me think she'd fractured a few bones. None of us tried to stop her. She finally let the cane drop from her hand, her breath sawing in and out of her lungs.

I went to her, placing my hand on her shoulder. "You feel any better?"

She held up her hand, pinching her finger and thumb together. "Tiny bit."

"Then… you tell us what you want to happen to

him, and we'll see that it's done. You have my word we'll do everything as you say. You should go home and rest."

She tipped her head back to stare up at me. "I'm not leaving. I'm not some shy, timid woman. Men terrify me because of him and the others I met after I ran away. But it all started with him."

"He killed your mom," Dad said.

"And I'm not your stepsister. I'm your half-sister." Joon smirked. "He loved my mom and only tolerated yours as a way to advance his career."

Nari's eyes filled with unshed tears. "You really did kill my mom?"

"Not by myself," he muttered, glaring at his wife.

Ah. Yes, it seemed Mrs. Kwon was far from innocent. Of course, I'd already known that. A little more dirt wasn't going to hurt at this point. She already wasn't leaving here alive.

Nari slowly turned her head to stare at her stepmother. I felt every muscle in her body tense. She shook with pure rage as she broke away from me and stalked closer to the woman. After holding her gaze for a few minutes, she glanced over at my dad and nearly ran to him. I didn't realize what she was after until she had his knife in her hand. The blade was nearly the length of her forearm. In her hands, it looked more like a short sword than a hunting knife.

Nari slashed Mrs. Kwon's face with the blade, slicing open both cheeks. Blood ran freely. The woman didn't make a sound.

"You awful, murdering, traitorous bitch! What did my mother ever do to you?" Nari demanded.

"She was in my way. The goal was for her to marry your father, help him gain a higher position in the Jo-Pok, then we'd frame her for cheating and he'd demand a divorce. But your saint of a mother didn't make it easy. So, I befriended her and started slipping poison in her tea."

"You're one of the most despicable people I've ever met." Nari plunged the knife into Mrs. Kwon's abdomen. The woman sputtered and coughed up a little blood. My sweet little wife had fire in her gaze as she yanked the blade free, then stabbed her again. Once she started, she couldn't seem to stop. After the eighth time, Mrs. Kwon's head slumped and she stopped breathing.

"Little chick, she's dead," Dad said.

She handed his knife back to him, and I pulled her into my arms. "Will you please go with Bones now? Take a shower and get into bed. I'll be home once we're done here."

"All right. Be careful." She tipped her face up and I leaned down to kiss her. Once she'd left the building, I shared a look with my dad. Neither of us had expected such a thing from her.

"Are you proud?" my dad asked Mr. Kwon. "You turned that innocent girl into a killer. You and your hell-bitch wife, and your foul younger daughter. All the good traits in Nari must have come from her mother."

"And I'm guessing her viciousness came from her mother's family," I said. I didn't understand anything about the Jo-Pok structure, but I had a feeling Nari's grandparents had been near the top. Possibly still were. I wasn't sure I wanted to meet them.

"Just finish it," Mr. Kwon said. "I already know you aren't going to let us live."

I glanced at Joon then back at him. "She's your favorite right? Your precious little girl who gets whatever she wants?"

He didn't say anything, but I could tell I had his attention. I grabbed a pair of pliers off a nearby table and approached Joon. Gripping her wrist, I used the tool to yank her fingernails off one at a time. She screamed and thrashed, calling me all sorts of names before pleading and offering me anything I wanted. After the last nail came off, I gripped her knuckle with the pliers and tightened them as much as I could while twisting. The joint popped and bulged as the bones broke.

"She liked to hear Nari's scream, didn't she?" I asked, looking over at Mr. Kwon. Tears ran down his cheeks as he stared at Joon. "Is it pretty? Hearing Joon's screams? Did Nari beg as much as this little whore? You heard what she offered. Every man in this club could use her however we wanted, as long as we didn't hurt her anymore."

"Not my style," Menace said. "But... I know some people."

I glanced over at him. "Who the fuck have you been hanging out with other than us?"

He shrugged. "Few gang members I met when I was a kid. They were a bit older than me. Now they're at the top of the food chain."

I focused on Joon again. "What did you have planned for Nari?"

She sneered at me. "Sanders promised to break her in real good. Said he'd shove his cock in all her holes, then let his friends do the same. Once they'd had their fun, he was going to slit her throat and watch her bleed out."

"Did you help him plan it?" I asked.

"Of course. Although I asked for a little special treatment in addition to what he wanted to do." Joon spat on the floor. "He was going to make sure she was torn up inside. It's what he promised me."

"I've met a lot of truly fucked-up people in my life," Dad said, "but you are one of a kind. And I don't mean that in a good way."

"I'll make a call," Menace said. "Well, two. I'll need permission from Titan, but everything she planned for Nari can happen to her. Right here."

"Do it," Dad said. "But one of us stays to make sure she's dead when it's over."

"Fine. I'll stand guard outside the door." Menace stepped out as he pulled his phone from his pocket.

I eyed Mr. Kwon. There were so many things I wanted to do to him, but as much as he adored Joon, I knew watching what would happen to her would be a far worse punishment. I took Dad's knife and used it to leave small cuts up and down his legs, over his torso and back, and on the soles of his feet. He bled freely, but not enough for him to bleed out anytime soon. In fact, the bleeding would slow and the wounds would crust over.

Dad picked up a metal bat off the table and went over to Mr. Kwon. He slammed it into both knees, and I knew he'd shattered them on impact. Whatever Nari had done before paled in comparison. The man let out a scream that would have done a horror movie actress proud. Dad continued to beat him with the bat until he hung limp, all the fight drained from him.

"Titan approved it," Menace said as he came back in. "The boys will be here soon. Any special instructions?"

"Just let them torture her the way she'd wanted Sanders to hurt Nari and slit her throat when they're done. As for Mr. Kwon… let him watch," I said.

"And then?" Menace eyed the man where he hung from the hook. "We could leave him like that.

He'd eventually die. It would give him time to relive those moments until he drew his last breath."

"If someone can stand guard and let me know when he's finally dead, then I'm okay with that. Nari did what she came to do. I promised they would all die. Just help me keep my word to her," I said.

"Consider it done." Menace pointed to the door. "Better go check on her. She probably needs you right about now. Want photo evidence when they're both dead?"

"Sure. Just make sure it's encrypted first. Don't need that shit landing in the wrong hands."

He nodded. "I'll take care of it."

Dad and I went out to our bikes and headed home. As I pulled into my driveway, I realized he'd gone to his own house. I knew he'd want to reassure himself Nari was all right, so I decided to text him after I checked on her.

I found her curled up in our bed, already asleep. Beating her father and killing her stepmother must have worn her out both physically and emotionally. I reached out to smooth her hair back from her face and stopped. Shower first. No. Message Dad first. I snapped a picture of her and sent it to him, letting him know she'd made it home safely. Then I took the hottest shower I could stand. It was the blood that bothered me. Being in the room with those three had me feeling dirtier than ever before. I scrubbed until my skin turned red, then got out and dried off. Sliding into bed next to Nari, I pulled her into my arms and held her as she slept.

Nearly four hours later, I received confirmation Joon was dead. If it had been possible to revive her and make her live through it all again, I'd have done it. Two down. One to go. I knew Kwon would take at least another day or three before he'd finally succumb to his wounds and die. Once they'd all been disposed of, it would truly be over for Nari. She had a fresh start without worrying what her family might do to her.

"Sweet dreams, my precious wife," I whispered and kissed the top of her head. "It will all be over soon."

Epilogue

Nari
One Month Later

The final results of my tests were in, and the news wasn't entirely awful. I stared at the paper in my hands and went over the phone call in my head once more. Iron would be home any moment. What would he think about all this? We hadn't really discussed expanding our family since our first week together.

I heard the front door open and rushed to greet him. He flashed me a smile and a wink as he toed off his boots and placed them on the shoe rack.

"Is there a special occasion or are you just super happy to see me today?" he asked.

"It can't be both?" I asked.

"Hit me with it," he said.

"The doctor called. The tests show that I can technically get pregnant, but he said it wouldn't be easy to carry the baby to term. The scarring is really bad and could result in a miscarriage, but if we want to have children, then there's a slim chance we can."

He pulled me into his arms and held me tight. "Would it be dangerous for you?"

"Well, he said there could be some risks, especially if we wait until I'm older. But I think all pregnancies are like that. There's no guarantee everything will go smoothly even with someone who's perfectly healthy."

He didn't say anything for several moments, just held me close. No matter how many times he said he didn't care whether or not we could have children, it still felt as if I would be disappointing him if I took the possibility away from him completely. We hadn't been together very long. Even if we did start a family, I thought this would be a little too soon.

"Why aren't you saying anything?" I asked.

"Trying to gather my thoughts for a moment. There's something I want to say but I'm not sure how you'll take it."

"Well, that doesn't sound the least bit ominous," I said with a bit of sarcasm in my tone.

"It's nothing bad. I know you were raised to believe that women had certain roles, such as maintaining the home and having children. It doesn't mean I feel that way. In fact, I was just considering the possibility of getting a vasectomy."

"Wait. What? Why would you do that?"

"You're the most important person to me. If getting pregnant could cause any problems or would most likely end with a miscarriage, then it would be better if you never got pregnant at all. I'm not trying to be an insensitive asshole. And I'm not saying that I never want a family with you."

"Then what exactly are you trying to say?" I asked.

"There are so many kids in the world who need a home. Some might be babies and others might be teenagers. The point is that we don't have to have a child the traditional way. If and when we decide to start a family, we can take in someone who has nowhere else to go and no one to love them. Wouldn't that be better?"

"Are you thinking about the children my father brought here illegally and forced to work for him until he sold them?"

He nodded. "Some of the kids aren't able to go back to their countries or their families. A lot of the boys went to criminal organizations who will raise them and turn them into soldiers. Out of the handful who have nowhere to go, Patriot and MaryAnne are going to take in one of them. There's a little boy who was only five years old and doesn't even know his own name. The hackers discovered his family is dead. The only way they were able to find him was through the records your dad kept, and it's possible it was a false lead. Either way, it's all we have to go on. Sending him back to his country isn't in his best interest. He's going to live with them now and be part of their family. So, if we ever decide we want children, then we can give a home to someone like that little boy."

"Why is it taking so long for them to get the little boy?" Where had he been the past month?

"Another club has been keeping him, and any others who weren't taken by the Jo-Pok, Yakuza, or anyone else. He's safe. The Swift Angels is a club full of first responders. Luckily, they're sometimes willing to look the other way when bad guys go missing, as long as they know why. We were lucky they decided to help."

"How can anyone call you cold? You have the biggest heart of anyone I've ever met. I'm so proud to be able to call myself your wife. Every day you say or do something that amazes me."

He shook his head. "I'm not anything special. So don't go putting me on a pedestal. Otherwise, I might fall off."

I went up on my tiptoes to kiss him. I didn't care what he said, or anyone else, for that matter. To me, Iron was perfect. Yes, he had a darker side and didn't shy away from killing someone he felt deserved it, but he treated me better than anyone ever had. Hearing him talk about the kids who needed homes made me realize he was right. I didn't have to give birth to a baby for it to be ours. If there was a little boy or girl out there who needed someone to love them, then I'd welcome them with open arms.

"Thank you for coming to talk with me that first day," I said. "I have to admit, Titan scared me. I'd only accepted the ride from Crow out of desperation. When he wouldn't drop me off somewhere in town and brought me here, I worried I'd only landed in another bad situation. Then I met you."

"I love you, Nari. You're the best thing that ever happened to me. Even better than finding out I have a sister. Just don't tell Roe I said that."

I smiled and hugged him. "I'll take it to my grave."

"Yeah, well… it better be a long-ass time before you need one. Not sure I can figure out how to survive without you."

"You were doing just fine before we met," I said. Unlike me. My life had been one terrible experience after another. I could genuinely say Iron had improved my life.

"No. I was existing," he said. "Sure, I get along with Roe and I love her. Dad and I have been trying to find our footing around each other. Or rather, I was. He was ready to welcome me as part of his family the moment he heard I was his son. I wasn't quite as happy about it."

"We have the best family ever," I said. "I can't wait to see Roe's babies."

"Not much longer."

I thought about the things we'd bought for them. Finding out she was having twins had been a surprise for everyone, but I knew if anyone could handle it, it would be Roe. She was going to be the best mother. The way she treated the kids around the compound was enough to show she was meant for motherhood.

"We should tell your dad," I said. "About me not having children. I know he's eager to be a grandpa. Roe's kids will distract him for a bit, but eventually, he'll ask when we're going to have some. Better for him to know now."

"I'll call him in a bit. Right now, I want to shower and change, then you and I are going to have a lazy afternoon and evening. Movies with snacks, and we'll order out for dinner. I don't want anything to distract us from spending time together."

"That sounds wonderful," I said.

"I do have a question. You know Wizard was able to figure out who your grandparents are on your mother's side. Do you want to contact them?"

"Not right now. Part of me is curious about them, and about my mother's life before she died. But at the same time, they're part of the Jo-Pok, and I don't want to invite trouble to our door. I don't know anything about them. They could decide they don't like us being married and try to hurt you or kidnap me."

"I think you're overreacting," he said. "However, it's your decision. I'll tell Wizard to sit on the information for now."

"Wait. Do they already know about me?" I asked. I couldn't remember having ever met them before. Did my mom ever talk to them after she married my dad?

"They do. They weren't aware you'd moved to America. Your father hid you from them. No idea why when he clearly didn't want you in his life, and I know it hurts to hear that but it's the truth. You may have been better off if he'd given you to them."

"No." I reached up to tug on his beard. "If they'd taken me in, then I never would have met you. How could that ever be better? No matter what I suffered, in the end that road led me here. I love you, Jack, and I want to spend the rest of my life with you. All I need is you and our family."

He nodded. "Fair enough. Go pick a movie. I'll be back in ten minutes. Oh, and lock the damn doors. I don't want that precious family you keep mentioning to come barging in."

I smiled as he walked off to go shower. He might act all grumpy as if they were an inconvenience, but I knew secretly he loved having them around. Even his dad. My biker might be cold and surly to other people. He might even scare people around town just by his very presence. They were all idiots. None of them bothered to truly look at him. The man had a heart of gold, and the gentlest touch.

I might have thought I was on the road to hell most of my life, but it turned out I'd found heaven at the end of the path... and I was going to do whatever it took to hang on to my new family and my husband. They'd shown me what love truly was, and what it felt like to be part of something special. Without them, I'd still be lost. Iron hadn't just physically saved me. He'd help heal my heart and my soul. I only wished he realized how amazing he truly was.

Blades (Devil's Fury MC 14)
A Dixie Reapers Bad Boy Romance
Harley Wylde

China -- I came to the US to further my education. I never counted on falling for a gruff biker who was so much older than me. But Blades never hesitated when I told him I was pregnant. He was the best man I'd ever met... until he went to prison. All our lives unraveled after that. My daughter was taken from me, and I was sold. I thought I'd never escape the hell of being exploited and abused, until he walked through the doors again, looking like a wrathful angel. He may have saved me, but do I really deserve his love?

Blades -- Being falsely accused of murder was bad enough. Finding out someone stole my woman and daughter was another. Our precious little Meiling found herself a good man, and she's safe. Now I need to save her mother. My China. I'm going to gut everyone who dared to touch her and send them all straight to hell... then I'll do whatever it takes to prove to her she's safe with me, and that I've never stopped loving her. China and Meiling are my entire world, and I'm going to protect them -- this time.

Prologue

The beautiful woman in the kitchen smiled at me, tucking her hair behind her ear. I'd never met anyone like her in all my life, and I still didn't know how the hell she was mine. But she was. She chopped the vegetables to add to the stir-fry she'd been prepping for lunch.

"Stop staring," she said.

"Can't help it. When I see something gorgeous, I just have to look."

She huffed at me. "When you say things like that, it makes me want to put blinders on you."

"Why?"

"So you can't look at other pretty women."

I grinned and moved closer, placing my hand on her hip. Our daughter cried from the next room, and I pulled away. China reached out to wrap her fingers around my wrist.

"I can get her," I said.

"I know, but you spoil her. Let her cry another minute. If she won't stop, then you can go get her."

I didn't know shit about raising kids. What I did know was that my daughter was the most beautiful baby ever. She had red hair like mine, blue eyes, and looked like a miniature version of her mother. China insisted her blue eyes would change color as she got older. Something about all babies having blue eyes. I'd never heard of such a thing and had no idea if it was true or not.

"Fine. How long do I have to wait? A full minute? Or can I go now?"

She rolled her eyes at me. "Go. I know I can't hold you back. It's like wrestling a bear."

I flashed her a smile and hurried off to our

daughter's room. I'd gotten them this small two-bedroom house so we'd have a place to be together as a family. The last thing I wanted was for my club to find out about China or Meiling. The Devil's Fury wasn't the right place for them. I had no doubt our asshole of a president would want to initiate China, and I was never going to let that happen.

I lifted my baby girl from her crib and held her against my chest. Her cries immediately stopped as she snuggled into me. My precious little angel! Carrying her back to the kitchen, I sat at the table with her while China finished making lunch.

"I have a job I need to do soon," I said. "Might mean I'm gone for a few days."

Honestly, it wasn't a job out of town, but if I didn't stick to the clubhouse for a night or two, my club would get suspicious. The thought of fucking other women sickened me. China was my one and only, but I couldn't keep her safe if I didn't play a certain role. I'd let the whores suck me off and pretended to take them somewhere to fuck them. Usually I got them off with my fingers and made sure they were happy enough to keep their mouths shut about how little I did with them.

Until her, cheating wouldn't have bothered me. Hell, I hadn't had a woman before China. The club pussy had always been enough. I hadn't seen the point in settling down. Now I had a woman and daughter I wanted to protect. Only reason I hadn't married China was so my club wouldn't find her. I didn't want too big of a paper trail linking the two of us together. I'd even given her the cash to pay for this place so it wouldn't be in my name.

She didn't say anything to my comment, but I noticed the slight tension in her body. She knew what it meant when I wasn't here, and I knew she hated it. Hell, I did too, but there was no walking away from the Devil's Fury. Only way out was to die. Or be stripped of my colors, which was pretty much the same thing. They'd do their best to kill me if it came to that.

I kissed Meiling's cheek. "Daddy has to go somewhere for a bit, but I'll hurry back as soon as I can. Will you miss me?"

She waved a chubby fist in the air and I smiled down at her. Never in my life had I seen anything more precious.

"You know we always miss you," China said. She finished cooking our food and set the plates on the table. I'd become a pro at eating with one hand while holding our daughter. I got to spend so little time here, I always held on to her as much as I could during my visits. In a perfect world, we'd spend every day together.

"I'd change things if I could," I said. "I've told you what the club is like. It's no place for either of you. This is safer."

She nodded. "I know. It doesn't mean I have to like it."

"China, I love you. Both of you mean everything to me. Give me some time. I'll try to come up with a better solution, but for now, this is it."

She sighed and started to eat. I hated seeing the sadness in her eyes. I wanted to take all her pain away, not cause her more.

After we ate, I handed Meiling off to China and kissed them both. "I have to go."

"I know. Please be safe, Robert."

She was the only one who called me by my real name. To everyone else, I was Blades. It always warmed my heart to hear my name on her lips, especially with her accent. I loved listening to her speak. Hell, I just loved everything about her.

I went outside and walked two blocks to my bike. Pulling my cut from my saddlebags, I put it on and started up the engine. Time to go back to reality and leave my slice of heaven behind. Another few days, and we could be together again.

The Pres was waiting for me at the clubhouse when I pulled up. I hadn't even had a chance to get off my bike before cops were pulling in, surrounding me. I eyed the Pres, wondering what the hell was going on.

"Nothing I can do about this, Blades. You either go with them, or they're going to tear this place apart."

Shit. I had a feeling this was going to delay me getting back to my girls. But the Pres wanted me to turn myself over to the police for some reason, so I'd do it. One of them approached with cuffs in his hands.

"Robert Young, you're under arrest for the murders of…"

Everything sounded like static after those words. Murder? Who the fuck had I killed? I eyed the Pres, who remained silent. His eyes said for me to go along with it. I didn't know what the hell was happening, but I didn't have a choice. He wanted me to protect the club, and I needed to keep my girls out of his sight.

The officer cuffed me and shoved me into the back of a squad car. As they drove off, I had a bad feeling. One that festered as the days passed. By the time my court date came around, I felt numb inside. My club had clearly abandoned me, and my woman and daughter had no idea what was going on. Although, it was possible she'd seen something on the news.

The judge sentencing me to life in prison for

multiple counts of murder hit me like a sledgehammer. My life was over. No more China. No more Meiling. At this point, I wasn't too broken up over not seeing my club again. They were my brothers, but I had something more important in my life now. A family. My true family.

If I'd known what would happen, I'd have fought harder.

Chapter One

Blades
Eighteen Years Later

I eyed the man in front of me. It had been a long ass time since I'd seen the Devil's Fury cut. "So, one of you finally came to see me. No one's ever brought a pretty woman with them, though."

The name *Dingo* wasn't one I was familiar with. Then again, he looked young. Probably started prospecting after I'd been locked up. He put his hand on the woman's shoulder and gave it a squeeze.

"You're Robert Young?" she asked.

"Don't go by that name anymore. I'm Blades. Who's looking for Young?"

She took a breath and seemed to be steeling herself. I should have been the one preparing. Her next words would have knocked me on my ass if I'd been standing.

"I'm Meiling Shan Young. Your daughter, if my birth certificate is correct."

I fell back against the metal chair. My daughter? "Fucking hell."

"So you do know who I am?" she asked.

"Yeah. Told your mother not to bring you here. Why did she let you come now?" In all this time, China had stayed away just as I'd demanded. Had something happened to bring my daughter here after all these years?

"She didn't. I don't even remember her," Meiling said.

My gaze shot to Dingo. Who the hell was he? Why had he brought her here? "Are you responsible for her being here? How she'd get mixed up with the club? I told Xi-wang to keep away from the Devil's

Fury."

"We don't know yet what happened to Xi-wang. Shortly after you were locked up, your daughter went into foster care and her mother vanished without a trace," Dingo said. "As to why she's with me... she's my wife."

I shot to my feet. "Like fuck she is!"

After everything I'd been through to keep them safe, this had to happen? I didn't know how she'd met this bastard, but I'd see to it he was buried six feet under. How dare he touch my precious child?

"Sit down, old man," Dingo said. "She's been accepted by the club as my ol' lady, and we're legally married. Besides, she could be carrying your grandchild."

I felt my blood pressure rising and wanted nothing more than to wring his neck. Slowly, I took my seat. Going after him right now wouldn't do me any good. If my daughter liked him, then it would only hurt my relationship with her -- assuming I ever had the chance to have one.

"Why the fuck are you here?" I asked, focusing on Dingo.

"We need some answers. Mei doesn't remember her mother, and never knew about you. In fact, her birth certificate was buried and a false one put in its place. You tried to keep her a secret, but it's time to talk."

I didn't like it, but they weren't the only ones who needed answers. They said my daughter couldn't remember her mother. Where the hell was China? If I found out someone had hurt her, I was going to slaughter everyone responsible. "Fine. I'll tell you what I know, then you explain what's really going on."

I told them how I met Meiling's mother, about us

falling in love, and me keeping the two of them a secret from the club. Everything up until I went to prison. After that, I lost track of China. I'd thought she was only listening to me and keeping away as I'd told her to do. I should have found a way to check up on her.

Meiling slumped in her seat. "So you don't know what happened to her, or how I ended up in foster care?"

"Nope. I never even heard she was missing. No one ever came to ask me about you, but you were mine legally. If someone finds out what happened, I sure the fuck want to know," I said.

"Outlaw is working on it," Dingo said. "He's a hacker for the club. Only thing we know for sure is the foster family who had Meiling..." Dingo stopped mid-sentence.

I wanted to ask what the hell a hacker was, but more importantly, what was it he didn't want to tell me? If it had to do with my daughter, then I deserved to know. He might be married to her, but she was my baby first and foremost.

Meiling met my gaze. I knew whatever they were hiding would gut me. "He doesn't want to tell you."

"Did they hurt you?" I asked.

"They made her into a whore by the age of fourteen," Dingo said. Even I could hear the pain in his voice.

I slammed my fists into the table, and everything went red. I roared out my rage, standing so fast the chair fell over. I ripped the chain free of the table and continued to pound the metal surface, denting it. Guards rushed in, and I knew they were going to put me in solitary if I didn't calm down, but I couldn't. I wanted to make them all suffer. Every last person who'd harmed my baby needed to die, and I wanted to be the one to do it.

Dingo held up a hand, cautioning them to stay back. "Give him a minute. We gave him bad news."

Bad news? I nearly laughed. That was putting it mildly. Finding out my favorite motorcycle had turned to rust would be bad news. Discovering my China had moved on and found someone else would be bad news. Hearing someone turned my daughter into a prostitute while she was still a kid made me want to set the entire world ablaze.

"No. Fuck that shit." I looked from my daughter to Dingo. "I didn't fucking kill those people. You find out who did, get me out of here, and I'll handle the men who hurt my daughter."

"I didn't hear that," one of the guards muttered. "Did. Not. Fucking. Hear. It." He walked out, dragging the other one with him. At least they had some sense.

"Are you trying to say you're innocent?" Meiling asked.

I gave a bark of laughter. Innocent? Me? Not hardly. "No, daughter. I'm far from innocent, but I didn't commit the murders I was accused of. If Outlaw can find out what happened with your situation, then maybe he can help with mine. When I got locked up, there wasn't anyone capable of digging up that kind of dirt, not within the club, and certainly no one who gave a shit about me. You get me out of here, and I'll make sure they all fucking pay."

"On one condition," Dingo said.

He had some nerve adding a stipulation. Was he trying to keep me away from my daughter?

"What's that, boy?" I asked.

"You give your blessing for me and Mei to be together." He cleared his throat. "I love her, and I will love and protect any children we have together. If we're ever blessed with any."

"You're an idiot," Mei told him, but I saw the affection in her gaze. "But I love you too."

The way he smiled at the words told me enough. The bastard was head over heels for my little girl, and since they were already married, I might as well learn to live with it.

"Fine. You have my blessing, as long as you make her happy. Fuck up, and I'll Goddamn bury you where they'll never find your body," I said.

The look he gave me assured me we were on the same page. I hoped like fuck the club was a better place than it had been when I got locked up. If it wasn't, I'd need to find a way to get Meiling away from there. It didn't matter if she was married to this little shit or not. I'd do whatever it took to keep her safe. I'd failed her until now. Never again.

"I know I'm a stranger to you, girl, but I'm your dad. I get out of here, and I'll make things right for you. I don't expect you to call me anything other than Blades, until I've earned the right to be called anything else."

"We'll have to agree to disagree," Meiling said. "Daddy."

I felt my throat grow tight and my eyes stung. I flashed her a smile, hoping she knew how much it meant for me to hear her call me Daddy. I'd missed out on everything. Her first steps. First words. And because I hadn't been there to keep them safe, someone had tried to destroy my family. Once I was free of this place, I'd seek retribution. I only hoped it didn't take them too long.

My daughter came closer and put her arms around me. I knew we weren't supposed to touch but fuck all of them. I hugged her tight, wanting to remember this moment forever.

"Love you, Meiling. Always have," I said, my voice a littler gruffer than usual. "Even if I can't get out of here, remember that. You were wanted, and you were loved. Never doubt it for a moment."

"Thank you, Daddy."

* * *

I hadn't realized they would have me freed within twenty-four hours. I'd spent eighteen years in prison for something I didn't do. All this time, I'd thought my woman was safe. Off living her life, providing for our child. How could I have been so wrong? I knew about the evil in the world. Faced it every fucking day, even before I'd gotten locked up. It never once crossed my mind that darkness would touch my two girls, especially since I'd made sure to keep them away from the club.

It had taken a month to handle all the people who'd hurt my daughter and to find my precious China. She'd been dumped in a brothel not too far over the state line. From what the hackers had found, it looked like she was still there. If she wasn't, I'd beat the hell out of everyone until I got some answers. One way or another, I was bringing her home.

Pulling into the parking lot of the Silk Purse, my heart hammered in my chest. It would be my first time seeing her in so damn long. Did she even remember me? Had they completely broken her?

I got off the bike and headed inside. The moment I saw her my fucking heart broke. My beautiful girl was just as stunning now as she'd been before, even with the scars clearly visible on her face and arms, and a few silver threads in her hair. She gave me a slight bow as I drew closer, but her eyes never met mine.

"Welcome to the Silk Purse. What will be your

pleasure tonight?" she asked, her voice still holding the accent I'd so loved all those years ago.

"My pleasure?" I asked. She still didn't look up. "I came to take my woman home. Our daughter needs her."

She went still, completely frozen. Slowly, she lifted her head and her gaze locked with mine. The Xi-wang I'd known was there, but just barely. I could see her, but I could also see the road of pain she'd traveled while we'd been apart.

"Xi-wang."

"Robert?" she asked softly. "You went to prison for murder."

"Didn't do it." I reached for her, tugging her against me. "But I did kill a few people since then. They all deserved it."

I stroked her cheek and wished I could turn back the clock. She'd had my heart the moment we locked eyes that first time. I'd have given anything to keep her safe, and I'd failed. I'd failed both her and our daughter.

"The people who put you here have been dealt with," I said. "They also were responsible for turning our daughter into a whore. I still don't know the entire story, but it seems the family she was with last has been part of a child pornography ring for decades. Family business, of all the fucked-up things. Any kids in the area who weren't white or fully white were flagged. When the pedophile making the videos got requests for certain types of girls and boys of certain ages, then they'd be sent to him. Our daughter could have been sent to him much sooner, so there's a small blessing in all this fucked-up mess."

She flinched and looked away, but I turned her face back to mine.

"Xi-wang, never do that again. I know what you've been through, and it doesn't matter." I mean, it did in a sense. I couldn't stand the thought of people hurting her, or other men touching what was mine. Didn't mean I blamed her for any of it. She was a victim in all this. No matter what she'd been through, she was still my precious China. My woman. The love of my life.

"It does," she said. "I'm dirty."

Maybe I should have said all those thoughts out loud.

"No, you're beautiful. My stunning woman, the mother of my child, the only woman to ever have my heart."

Her eyes misted with tears and one slipped down her cheek. I brushed it away before kissing her softly. She resisted at first, but then I felt her arms come around my neck as she kissed me back.

"I love you, Robert," she said. "I fought, so hard. I was yours, only ever yours."

"It's time to go home, China."

She smiled at the name I'd always called her. But the smile slipped from her face as she touched her scars and looked at her surroundings. I could tell she was retreating, that she would refuse to come with me, and I couldn't let that happen. She belonged with me. If I'd not kept her from the club all those years ago, maybe none of this would have happened. Or maybe they'd have chewed her up and spit her out. Too late to second-guess myself now.

"You're mine. Do you hear me?" I asked.

"I want to be yours. In my heart, I always was."

My hold on her tightened. "You always have been and always will be my China. The love of my life."

She was still withdrawn, more than I'd have liked, but what I was seeing was more than I'd expected. I'd been led to believe that she was empty, dead inside. But my China was still there.

"Our daughter is married," I said. "To a member of my club."

Her gaze jerked to mine. "You said they were dangerous."

I snorted and looked around. "China, do you see where you are? Did you hear what I said happened to our daughter? Trust me. The club is the safest place for both of you. Things have changed since I went away. It's a good place to raise a family. *Our* family."

"They hurt her?" she asked.

"Yeah, honey. They hurt her bad, but she's healing. Dingo is good to her, worships her."

"She might need to talk, about what happened." Xi-wang locked her gaze with mine. "You think she'll accept me? That your club will?"

"They'll love you, just the way I do. There's a house. It's ours, but we'll have to make it a home. Think you're up for the task?"

She gave me a smile, a real one that gave me hope. "Okay. The owners won't like me leaving, though."

I pulled a knife and smiled. "They don't call me Blades for nothing, China. You let me handle the people who run this place. Go out and wait by my bike."

She nodded and paused only long enough to kiss my cheek. It looked like I would get a little bit bloody before I got to take my woman home, but she was worth the effort I'd have to put into finding a clean shirt.

"All right, you fuckers," I yelled out. "Who

wants to die first?"

I heard movement to my right and laughed. They could run, but they'd never make it. I stalked them through the building, finding one after another. The first was cowering in the corner like a little bitch. I hefted him to his feet, lifting him off the floor.

He kicked like a toddler and struggled to break free. Had he been one of the ones to touch her? Had he left any of her scars? Didn't matter. The fact he was still breathing pissed me off.

"You should have never taken her. China is mine. None of you had the right to put your filthy hands on hers."

"Who the fuck is China?" he asked, wheezing a bit as he struggled to breathe.

"Xi-wang."

"Didn't," he said in a strangled voice. "Never touched her."

"Really? You've never slapped her? Cut her? Left a bruise or verbally abused her?" I asked. "I find it hard to believe."

His eyes went wider with each word, and I knew I'd been right. Even if he hadn't put his cock inside her, he'd still hurt my precious China. There was only one place someone like him should be... hell. Without another moment of hesitation, I dragged my blade across his throat. He choked on his own blood as I dropped him back to the floor. One down. Didn't know how many others were left.

The second man tried to take me out. He leapt from the shadows, knife drawn. His hand trembled and the knife in his grasp shook. Fucking amateur. I may have been out of the game for a while, but this was seriously pathetic. These were the men they left in charge?

"Son, if you're planning to stab someone, make sure you're able to actually carry out your task."

I knocked the blade from his hand. As badly as I wanted to kill him, I wanted to make him suffer first. My fist landed against his jaw with enough force to knock him off his feet. Hauling him back up, I landed blow after blow until his face was nothing more than a bloody mess.

Gripping my knife, I sank it into his gut, watching as his eyes widened in shock. Just to be sure he took the express ride to Lucifer's domain, I stabbed him four more times.

A shot rang out and I ducked, putting my back to a wall. It sounded like it had come from the hallway up ahead. I made my way closer, gripping the handle of my knife tightly. Going low, I lunged around the doorway and sank my blade into the man's leg. He cursed and shot at me again. Thankfully, his aim fucking sucked.

I landed a punch to his chin and another to his abdomen, then knocked the gun from his hand. "How many others are there?"

He gasped and shook his head. I wasn't sure if he meant he was the last, or if he refused to tell me. I stabbed his other leg, and gave the knife a twist, making him squeal like a pig.

"Boy, don't make me ask again."

"None," he said. "There's no one else except the girls. Take them. Just let me live."

I snorted. Fat fucking chance. "The moment you put my woman to work in this place you sealed your fate."

Didn't matter if it had been him personally or his organization. To me, they were all the same. I sliced his throat and stood, eyeing my surroundings. The girls were all hiding. Not that I could blame them. Probably feared I was going to kill them too.

"The woman up front is my wife," I said. Small fib, but I'd make it real as soon as she'd let me. "I came here to bring her home. These men abducted her. Hurt her. I'm sure they did the same with you. You're free to leave."

A door opened and a young Chinese girl poked her head out. "We're free?"

"Yeah, sweetheart. These people don't own you anymore. Get out of this place. Start a new life. Go home to your family. Whatever it is you want to do, go do it."

Another came from another room. "We don't have anywhere to go."

I pulled out the phone I'd recently gotten. "Anyone have a pen and paper?"

The first girl disappeared and came back with both, handing them to me. I wrote down Outlaw's name and number, then gave it back to her.

"What's that?" the second woman asked.

"He's part of my club, married with kids, and I know he'll help all of you. Give him a call and he'll find a place for all of you to stay. But I need everyone out of this building right now. I'm turning this bitch to nothing but ash."

More doors opened, and I stood back as half a dozen young Chinese girls hurried past, as well as several older ones. They each thanked me on their way by. I scoured the building and finally found what I was searching for. Some of the cleaning chemicals were highly flammable. I doused as much of the first floor as I could, then lit a match and tossed it.

China placed her hand in mine as we watched the place burn. "It's really over."

"Yeah, it is." I turned to her, tipping her face up. Without a moment of hesitation, I pressed my lips to hers. My cock went rock hard, and my heart raced in my chest. Kissing her now was every bit as potent as it had been all those years ago. "Love you, my China doll."

"You know, some people would find that offensive," she mumbled.

"Do you?" I asked. I didn't give a fuck about anyone else.

"I don't care what you call me. Just knowing you're alive, and we're together again, is more than enough. I'd answer to anything. But... I like that you call me China. No one else ever gave me a pet name."

"Then I'll call you China for the rest of my life. Let's go home to our daughter."

I led her over to my bike and helped her onto the back. With one last look at the burning building, I sped away. It was time for a new chapter in both of our lives. Maybe this time we'd get it right.

Chapter Two

China

Everything felt surreal. I'd spent so many years being used as a whore I wasn't sure how to be anything else. Seeing Robert again after all that time had been both the best and worst thing to ever happen to me. It shamed me, knowing I'd been forced to betray him. Having him find me in such a place had me wanting to run from him. How could he stand to look at me now?

I stared at my reflection in the bathroom mirror. Today had been surprising. I never thought I'd see Blades again, much less be rescued by him. He'd pulled off the highway on our way here so he could change his shirt and wipe the blood off his cut. Then he'd stopped at a store and bought me a change of clothes and shoes. The shift was soft, and the jade green color filled me with peace. The leggings stuck to me like a second skin but were more comfortable than I'd have thought. He'd grumbled about the ankle boots not being the sort a biker's woman should wear. I knew he'd chosen them because I'd worn something similar in the past and liked them.

From the moment he'd walked through the door of the Silk Purse, he'd done his best to set me at ease and let me know I was still wanted. I knew I should be grateful and feel honored he wanted to be with me after all this time. I'd seen the way women watched him, both in our past and now. He hadn't chosen me due to a lack of options. Although, I did worry he'd come to regret his decision. He should have left me where I was and started a new life without me.

Stepping out of the bathroom, I found him staring at the different snack foods. He'd already filled his bike with gas, and I had to admit I could eat. The thought of stuffing myself with chips, jerky, or whatever else filled the shelves made me wince. The Silk Purse had kept us fed, just not very well. I'd hoped for something at least hot if not nutritious. Although, I wouldn't be picky. He'd tracked me down, freed me, and was now taking me to our home.

I didn't know what had become of the place he'd gotten for us before. Since he'd been in prison, all our things were probably long gone. Pictures of us together, and our daughter's baby pictures. Items I'd brought with me from China, things my parents had given me. Of course, they'd disowned me when they found out I was pregnant and who Meiling's father was. I'd had to drop out of college and fend for myself. Or rather, Blades had taken care of me once I'd told him about our baby.

If only I had a way to find everything we'd lost… We'd shared so many precious memories before it all went incredibly wrong.

"As much as I'd like to hurry back to the compound, I should probably get you something to eat," he said. I tried to hide my grimace as I looked over the junk on the shelves, but I clearly didn't succeed. I heard him chuckle softly. "Not here, China. There's a diner just down the street. Saw it on my way to get you. It might not be the best food you've ever had, but it will be better than anything here."

"All right. If you're sure we have time," I said.

He took my hand and led me outside. After I got on the back of his bike again, wrapping my arms around his waist, he pulled out of the gas station parking lot and stopped midway down the next block. He found a place to park right outside the door of the diner and shut off his bike. We went inside, hand in hand, and I couldn't even begin to name everything I was feeling.

Tears burned my eyes when I thought of what we'd all suffered. If everyone had left us alone, could we have led a somewhat normal and happy life? I didn't think I'd ever feel clean again, and the thought of him touching me filled me with dread. Not because I'd hate it, but because I no longer felt worthy of him. It didn't matter what he said. I couldn't change the way I saw myself. Not right away. Hopefully, with time, I'd have the same confidence he'd instilled in me before. Being with him had always filled me with wonder. I'd experienced so many new things after we met.

"Sit anywhere you'd like," a woman called out.

He led me to a booth nearby and I sat across from him. A man at the next table turned to look at me, and my blood ran cold. Maybe we should have gotten farther down the road before we stopped. We might be one town away from the Silk Purse, but I knew this man. He'd been one of the regular clients.

"Since when do they let whores wander around freely?" he asked.

I saw Blades stiffen. His hand fisted on top of the table, and he stood. He wouldn't start a fight here, would he? If the police came, then he could go back to prison. I wanted to stop him, and yet... all I could do was watch in fear.

"What the fuck did you just say?" he asked.

"You heard me. Only thing she's good for is spreading her legs, if you're into old, used-up pussy like that." The man laughed as if he'd said the funniest thing in the world. Maybe if he'd been paying attention, he would notice he'd screwed up. "I like the younger ones myself. Nice and tight."

Blades hauled back his fist and slammed it into

the man's mouth. He fell off his chair, sputtering and spitting out blood, as well as three teeth.

"I hope your affairs are in order," Blades said.

"You can't hit me! I'm going to call the police," he said, puffing up as if he were actually someone important. If he were, I doubted he'd be wearing cheap clothes with stains on them.

"You don't need the police, asshole. You need the fucking coroner." Blades hit him again. When he landed a third blow, it knocked the man out cold.

A woman with an apron around her waist hurried over. "I kept telling that jackass sooner or later his mouth would get him into trouble."

"Sorry for the mess," Blades said, motioning to the blood and teeth on the floor.

"No need to apologize. Leonard tends to piss off just about everyone. I'll call his cousin to haul him home. At least this time he didn't pass out from being drunk off his ass," she said.

Blades retook his seat and I stared at him. "He only spoke the truth."

"No, the fuck he didn't. You're my woman, China. The mother of my child. Anyone calls you a whore, they'd better count themselves lucky if they live to see the next sunrise. I won't tolerate anyone speaking to you, or about you, like that."

The woman returned with a pad and pen in her hand. "What would you like to drink?"

Her calm in this situation amazed me. The man's words, and the fact Blades had knocked him out, didn't seem to bother her in the least. She'd said the man had a tendency to say things he shouldn't. How many people had he started fights with in the diner? Why hadn't she just banned him?

"Coffee for me," Blades said. "And maybe some

water."

At the Silk Purse, we'd only been permitted tap water. It had been so long since I'd had anything else to drink, I wasn't sure if my stomach could handle it. The meal alone might cause problems, after only eating bland fish and rice for most of my meals.

"Water for me as well," I said.

The woman wrote it down, reached over to the counter, and handed us two menus. "I'll get those out while you decide what you want to eat. Although, word of advice, stay away from the salads. The lettuce looked a bit wilted earlier."

Blades opened a menu and handed it to me before looking over his own. I didn't remember what most of this even tasted like or hadn't tried it before at all. I knew I hadn't liked hamburgers in the past, so I ignored those. When the woman returned, we both ordered our food, and then sat in a somewhat awkward silence.

Even though I hadn't seen him in eighteen years, my heart still raced when I looked at him. He'd aged well. Better than me. I looked at my hands and stared at the scars marring my skin. I had more hidden under my clothes. What would people think when they saw me? I wasn't sure how much his club knew about my circumstances. Discovering I'd been in a brothel was one thing. Understanding the level of suffering we'd all endured was another. Exactly how much did they know?

"The other girls... you're sure they'll be okay?" I asked.

"Yeah. Gave one of them Outlaw's number. He'll get them somewhere safe tonight and find people to help them." He shrugged a shoulder. "I don't know shit about computers so I don't understand how he'll do it. But that's how I was able to find you. He and his hacker friends tracked down every person responsible for your disappearance and what happened to our daughter."

"I'm scared, Robert. What if Meiling doesn't want me there? What if your club hates me?"

He reached over and took my hand. "First of all, our daughter is waiting impatiently for me to return with you. Finding out you were alive was some of the best news she's ever gotten. Second, my club will support you because you're mine. They're not the same as when I went to prison. Things have changed a lot."

"You said that before, but…" I wanted to believe everything would be okay. I really did. It didn't stop the feeling of dread that filled me.

Our food arrived and we ate while stealing glances at one another. The fact he'd come for me after all this time proved how much he still loved me. I only hoped he wouldn't be disappointed when he realized I wasn't the same woman he'd known before. Too much had happened for me to ever be that innocent. He'd been my one and only. Thinking about what those men had done to me soured my appetite and I set my fork aside.

"I know you aren't full," he said. "China, you need to eat. We still have a long trip ahead of us. Then when we get home, there will still be things you need. The food will give you energy. Please eat."

It was the *please* that did me in. He hardly ever said the word, so I knew he meant it. The fact I'd stopped eating really bothered him.

"What do I need to know before we get there?" I asked.

"Our daughter goes by Mei and her husband is Dingo. The club has new officers, or rather new to me.

Grizzly is in charge. You'll like him. He can be a bit intimidating, but from what I've seen, he's gentle with women and kids. When we're around other people, you'll need to remember to call me Blades. Doesn't matter when it's just us, or even if Meiling and Dingo are over."

"You said we have a house there already? But not the one you got for us before."

He nodded. "I'm not sure what happened to that one. Our new home isn't overly large, but it's bigger than what we had before. Enough space for us, and when we have grandchildren, they'll have a room for spending the night."

It all sounded nice. Almost a little too perfect. It still worried me that his club might not accept me. It wouldn't surprise me if he'd bullied them into letting me stay there. Once he got an idea in his head, he didn't let go. I'd loved his determination when we'd been younger. Right now, I wasn't sure if it was necessarily a good thing.

"The club has women who are wives and some who are old ladies. It doesn't have anything to do with their age, it just means they're in a committed relationship with one of my brothers but not in the legal sense." He took a swallow of his coffee. "Our daughter is married to Dingo. She also wears a property cut that says *Property of Dingo* on the back, which is what all the claimed women have."

"Are you saying I have to wear one?" I asked. After the things I'd been through since he went to prison, I wasn't sure I liked the thought of being labeled property. Was living with his club going to be any different from being sold to those men before? I knew Blades would keep me safe if he could. But I had to admit, despite how capable he seemed, he was getting older.

He shook his head. "No. I'm not going to force you to do something you don't want to do. Take time to adjust to living with me, get to know our daughter and the club, and we'll take it from there. Would I like for you to have one? Of course. It shows you're mine and gives you a layer of protection."

"I don't understand," I said.

"I know you don't. In time, you'll see how things work. People around town know who we are. Some will look down on us or our women, thinking we're nothing more than dirty bikers. Others show respect. We don't have to rush into things. We have all the time in the world."

Did we really? Neither of us were as young as we used to be. Most women my age were in better shape than me. Being sold and treated like less than a human being had aged me. If anyone were to guess my age, they'd probably add a decade. Then again, Blades was much older than me. It only made it seem as if there was a little less of a gap between us. I'd noticed the way people looked at us before.

We finished our meal and Blades paid. The rest of the trip to our new home left me feeling anxious. It felt like there was a heavy weight on my shoulders, and my stomach seemed to be tied into knots. He approached a gate and someone waved him through. The ride ended outside a cute home with a small front yard. He'd said it was a nice home and bigger than our last one, but I hadn't expected it to be so well-maintained. The size took me by surprise as well. This was more than a little bit bigger.

He held my hand as I got off, and my knees nearly buckled. It had been far too long since I'd ridden on his motorcycle. I still remembered our first ride together. It had been both terrifying and thrilling. I'd never done anything so exciting in my life.

"Ready to go inside?" he asked.

I gave him a nod and slowly approached the front door. It felt like people were watching me, but I hadn't noticed anyone outside near our house. I knew it was likely my imagination. He pushed open the door and motioned for me to enter first. I stepped in and removed my shoes, placing them next to the door. It was a habit I hadn't broken even all these years after moving from China. The pink slippers in my size made my eyes mist with tears.

"Did you think I'd forget?" he asked as he removed his own boots.

"It's been such a long time."

"There's not a damn thing I don't remember about you, Xi-wang. In my heart, you were my wife. If I hadn't been so worried about the club discovering you and our daughter, I'd have married you back then. Of course, then you'd have been stuck with a convict as a spouse."

I'd been shocked when I saw the news. Since no one had known about our relationship, there hadn't been a call or knock at the door to inform me he'd been locked up. He could have used his phone call when they first took him in, but I understood why he hadn't. If might have seemed suspicious to anyone tracking the people he contacted, and he'd needed a lawyer.

"I didn't believe what they said." I looked up at him. "The man who touched his daughter so gently, and said the sweetest things to me, couldn't have hurt all those people."

He snorted. "China, you just watched me knock someone out at the diner. You know damn well I killed the men inside the brothel before I set it on fire. I'm not a saint."

"You're a good man. I learned long ago sometimes good people have to do bad things in order to protect those they love." I reached up and placed my palm against his cheek. "I love you, Robert, and I know who you truly are."

He took my hand and kissed it. "Likewise. So no more thoughts of not being good enough, or whatever other silliness is in your head. You're a strong, incredible woman. And you're mine. Nothing else matters."

I didn't know how he could just sweep it all away as if it never happened. I'd do my best to heal and become the woman he saw and not the one I perceived myself to be. Right now, I felt a little out of place. I folded my arms around my torso and looked around our home. It seemed plain and had the bare minimum needed. I'd never been much for clutter, so I didn't mind.

"I haven't had this place long," he said. "We can decorate however you'd like."

"I'd like to take a shower," I said. Maybe the hot water would wash away the filth I felt all the way down to my soul, but I doubted it. I hadn't had a chance to get clean since leaving the Silk Purse, and I didn't like the idea of anything from that place still lingering on my skin and entering this house.

"I'll show you to our room. I couldn't find the shampoo you used to use, so you'll have to make do with what's in there right now. Same for the soap you liked. I only remembered the scent and not the name."

"It's fine."

His eyebrows rose at the word *fine* and I nearly smiled. He used to grumble whenever I said that, claiming it was a flat-out lie. It seemed he remembered a lot of things about me. It both made me feel warm inside, and sad. All the years we'd lost… I knew we couldn't get them back, but I wanted to make new memories with him. This was our chance for a fresh start. Whatever it took, I'd prove to him I still loved him and that I could stand by his side. I only hoped it didn't take me as long as I feared.

Chapter Three

Blades

I hated it when she tried to smile and make me believe everything was all right, when I damn well knew it wasn't. I could see the pain in her eyes, and the doubts. Even though I'd taken her from the Silk Purse, part of her still remained there. They'd beaten her, broken her down, and turned her into a shell of the woman I'd once known. If I looked hard enough, I could see the old China lurking inside, but I didn't know how long it would take before she surfaced fully.

While she started the shower, I gave her some privacy. Mostly because I had something I needed to do. Now that I knew what size clothes she wore, I placed an order for pickup at the local big box store, then I shot off a text to a Prospect to pick it up and gave him the confirmation number. She'd need another set of clothes when she finished washing.

I went out to my bike and pulled a sack out of the saddlebag. I'd made sure to get her an extra bra and several pair of panties. Taking the sack inside, I set them on the dresser. As quietly as possible, I approached the bathroom and listened to see if she seemed okay. The fact it was dead silent bothered me. Peering into the room, I saw her kneeling on the shower floor and scrubbing at her skin so hard it was turning red.

With a muffled curse, I stripped out of my clothes and went to join her. It's what I'd have done in the past. Tiptoeing around and pretending she hadn't had something awful happen wouldn't be doing her any favors. At the same time, the more things we did that were the same as before, I thought the faster she might realize she was safe, and I still loved the hell out of her.

I entered the shower and knelt down behind her, placing my hand on her back. Her long hair hung past her waist. I'd always loved her hair. "Sweetheart, you're going to rub your skin off if you keep this up," I said softly. "Let's stand up and I'll help you wash."

She gave a jerky nod and staggered to her feet. It took me a minute to stand, my knees cracking and popping. Getting old was a bitch. I took the soap from her and lathered my hands before smoothing the suds over her skin. She felt as soft as she had before, except for the ridges from her scars. Now that I'd seen her without clothes on, I could tell how badly they'd hurt her. At least, on the outside. I had no doubt the emotional damage had been far worse.

"Do you think we'd have been happy?" she asked, her voice breaking a little.

"You mean if I hadn't gone to prison and you hadn't been sold?"

She nodded. "Things were going well. I knew there was a part of your life I could never experience, but you came to us as often as you could. It wasn't perfect, but it was *our* life."

"I know, China. I'm so fucking sorry for all of it. Maybe if I'd fought harder when I'd been arrested, then I could have gotten out. Even though I knew I hadn't done the crimes they'd accused me of, I didn't have proof. If it weren't for Outlaw's friends, I'd still be in prison."

"And I'd still be a whore," she murmured.

"No. Fuck no! The club would have saved you, if for no other reason than you're mine and you're Meiling's mother. They'd have done the right thing. The crew I was with back then is another story. Some of them were twisted. I'm glad the Devil's Fury is different from what it used to be. They can help me protect my family now."

I finished washing her, wishing I could make my cock behave. At least she hadn't commented on it. She didn't look as distressed as before, and I hoped this helped her at least a little. I put my arms around her and held her close, offering what comfort I could. I knew it wouldn't be enough to make up for all the ugliness she'd faced, but it was the best I could do for now.

"I love you, Xi-wang." I hoped using her real name would make her realize how sincere my words were. Sure, I called her China because it was my nickname for her, and she'd always smiled when she heard it. This seemed to call for something a little more serious. "There's nothing in this world that will ever make me stop loving you. I've cherished you from the moment we met. You know that, don't you?"

She nodded against my chest but wouldn't look up. Since we were standing under the water, I had no idea if she was crying. I hoped like hell she wasn't. All I wanted was for her to smile, to find happiness, and find a way to leave the nightmare of her past behind. Being in prison hadn't been a party, but I'd had it far better than her.

"Someone is going to deliver some clothes to the porch in a little bit. I put your other new bra and panties in the bedroom. Why don't you dry off and put on one of my T-shirts for now?"

She sniffled and looked up at me. Yeah, my girl had been crying, and it fucking gutted me. I smoothed my fingers over her cheeks and leaned down to kiss her softly. Her breath hitched and she let out a little sigh.

"I want to wash you," she said, her cheeks

flushing a little.

"If you do that, I'm not sure I can control myself. It would be best to let me finish up alone," I said.

"I'm not afraid of you. Not once have you ever hurt me, Robert."

I placed the soap in her hand. "Then have at it, but just so you know, I have no control over the fact my cock reacts to you. So, ignore the fact I'm hard as a fucking post."

A slight smile tilted her lips on one corner, and it was the best damn sight I'd seen since I saved her from that hellhole. Her eyes flashed with a bit of mischief, and I loved seeing that little spark inside her. Maybe she wasn't quite as lost as I'd feared.

The moment she slid her soap-covered hands across my chest and down my ribs, a shiver ran down my spine. I hadn't felt anything this amazing since the last time I'd been with her. I watched her face as she washed me, and smiled when her cheeks went even pinker as her hand wrapped around my cock. Christ! The slightest shift in her hand and I was damn near ready to come. Of course, the last woman I'd been with had been her, and that was a long-ass time ago.

"I think that's clean," I said, my voice coming out raspier than before.

"Not yet." She slid her hand to the base of my cock, then down to cup my balls. I closed my eyes and groaned, wondering if she was trying to kill me. Did she not have any idea how badly I wanted her? Just not at the risk of causing her harm. "I'm clean."

I jolted and my eyes opened. "What?"

"I said I'm clean. I haven't been requested by a customer in several years, and we were all tested regularly. So if that's why you're holding back…"

I shook my head. "No, honey. That wasn't it. As

much as I want you, I don't want to cause you any pain. Like I said before, we have all our lives to be together. There's no rush."

"Robert…" She squeezed my balls and I winced. "I'm not a delicate flower. I won't break. How long has it been for you?"

"Since we were last together," I admitted.

"I wish I could say the same." The light in her eyes faded a little. "I want you to treat me as you always have. Is that asking too much?"

"No, it's not. Are you sure this is what you want? Neither of us is as young as we used to be. There's a perfectly good bed in the other room."

This time her smile lit up her face and she laughed softly. "Are you saying you're too old to have sex in the shower?"

I gave her a low growl and backed her to the wall. The water ran over my shoulders and rinsed the soap from my body as I leaned in closer to her. "Guess I better prove I'm still capable. Is that what you're saying?"

She nodded. Her eyes darkened with hunger, and I couldn't hold back anymore. I kissed her until we were both breathless, my lips devouring hers. Lifting her, I urged her legs around my hips and lined up my cock with her pussy. My heart hammered in my chest, and I had to remind myself to go slow. Easing into her, my jaw clenched, and I wondered how long I'd last. She felt so tight and wet. So fucking perfect.

"Better hold on, China. This is probably going to be a fast, hard ride."

She tugged on my beard. "That was always the best kind."

I slid all the way in and closed my eyes, pressing my forehead to hers. Home. That's what this felt like…

I finally felt like I'd come home because that's what China was to me. I drew my hips back and thrust into her again. She clung to me, her nails biting into my skin. Her lips parted and I couldn't resist kissing her once more.

Our tongues tangled as I fucked her against the shower wall. Less than a dozen strokes and I knew I was about to blow, but my beautiful woman hadn't yet. I wasn't about to leave her behind. Reaching between our bodies, I played with her clit, pinching and rolling it between my fingers. She gasped and arched into me.

"Yes, Robert! Please don't stop."

"Never. Come for me, China. Come all over my cock. Show me how much you missed me, missed *this*."

My words triggered her orgasm, and she called out my name. The heat of her release was enough to push me over the edge. I pounded into her until every last drop of cum had been wrung from my balls. Panting for breath, I eased from her body and helped her stand again. It only took a few minutes for us to both clean up and get out of the shower.

The rosiness in her cheeks and the brightness of her eyes made me realize she'd needed that as much as I had. It was our first time together in nearly two decades. As much as I'd have liked for it to last longer, or to have been more romantic, for us it was perfect.

She put on another pair of her new panties, then pulled on one of my shirts. It fell nearly to her knees, reminding me of how petite she was. She'd always been tiny, although it bothered me that she'd lost weight since I'd last seen her. As far as I was concerned, she hadn't had any to lose. Now I could clearly see her ribs and hip bones. It would take some time to put weight back on her, but I knew it would happen with enough healthy meals.

"Want to watch TV?" I asked.

"Sure. I'll let you pick. Just don't be offended if I fall asleep."

"Tired?" I smoothed her hair back, then pulled her into the bathroom again. Running a comb through the long tresses, I braided it for her, like I'd done when we were younger. I pulled a hair tie from the drawer and fastened it around the end.

"I am," she said. "Why do you have those?"

"One of the things I prepared for you. There's also your favorite lip balm, some hair clips, and some clear nail polish along with remover."

"You made it sound like you didn't have anything for me here at the house." She looked up at me. "How did you know I'd still be there, or that I'd come with you? What if I'd been too broken?"

"I'd have brought you home regardless because this is where you belong. Here with me, and our daughter. You know Meiling wants to see you."

She nodded. "I know. I'm not ready yet. Please ask her to wait a little longer."

I kissed her forehead. "I will."

We went to the living room and settled on the couch. I flipped on the TV and put on a show I thought she might enjoy. But it seemed she really had been exhausted. It hadn't been on more than fifteen minutes before she was sound asleep.

I watched her more than the TV, marveling at the fact she was really here. Never again would I let anything happen to her. Nothing would separate us other than death, and even then, the Grim Reaper had better fucking think twice. China was mine, and I was damn sure not letting her go.

Chapter Four

China

I was hiding like a coward and I knew it. I'd been home with Blades for several days now, and I still hadn't seen our daughter. No matter how much Blades said she wanted to see me, I still felt pure fear she'd reject me. I'd been absent for most of her life and had failed to protect her when she was small. What if she resented me? What if she was ashamed to have a mother like me?

Blades placed his hands on my shoulders and gave them a slight squeeze. "It's time, China. I've tried to be patient, and I've waited for you to tell me you're ready. In good conscience, I can't tell our daughter no one more time."

"But…"

"No, China. Enough is enough. Meiling isn't going to call you names, look at you like you're some sort of monster, or treat you badly. If anything, she feels like you don't want to see her because there's something wrong with *her*."

I winced. That was the last thing I'd wanted. Blades seemed to have a good relationship with her. If she'd accepted him, even knowing he'd gone to prison, then maybe I didn't have to worry about her accepting me.

"All right. Invite her over," I said.

"Proud of you, China." He kissed the top of my head. "And I already called her this morning. She'll be here any minute."

"What?" I turned to stare up at him. "Why would you do that before talking to me?"

"Because you need to see her. It's not something you can put off indefinitely. You'll also need to meet the rest of the club soon. They're part of my family as well, and I know they'll support you. None of them care about your past, China. Not in the way you're worried about. They don't like what happened to you, but they don't think less of you because of it."

I knew he was right. He'd been so patient with me and understanding. It was time for me to be brave and face this new life head-on. I'd thought it would be easier with him by my side. Until it came time to make the decision to see Meiling. I always chickened out. Now it had been taken out of my hands.

"Dad," a voice yelled out from the front of the house.

"Take off your shoes," he shouted back. "We're in the kitchen."

"I should have made something," I said. "I don't have anything to offer her."

"I'm not here for food," Meiling said. I spotted her just inside the kitchen doorway and stared, tears blurring my vision. "Hi, Mom."

I pressed my hand to my mouth to hold back my sobs. Sagging against Blades, I wasn't sure I could remain standing. My knees felt weak, and the world spun a little. My baby girl was all grown up, and incredibly beautiful. She looked like a younger version of me, except for her father's red hair and green eyes. It felt like a wrecking ball slammed into me when I thought of all the things I'd missed over the years, and how much we'd both suffered.

Meiling came closer and I opened my arms to her. She hugged me so tight. I held her close as I cried, and only after a few minutes did I notice the man standing several feet behind my daughter. I tensed and pulled away.

"It's okay, China," Blades said. "This is Dingo,

our son-in-law. He treats our Meiling like a princess."

"It's nice to meet you," Dingo said. "Um, I'm not really sure what to call you."

I glanced at Blades before holding Dingo's gaze again. "He calls me China. My name is Xi-wang. Whatever you're more comfortable with."

"He married me to save me," Meiling said. "My friend Beau technically brought me here, but Jameson stepped up and did whatever it took to keep me safe. It didn't take long for me to fall for him. He's a really good man."

"Jameson?" I asked.

Dingo nodded. "It's my real name. I'm sure Blades already talked to you about how that part of the club works? Dingo is my road name, and the only one I use around the club or even in town."

"Yes, a little. I'm still confused on some things, but I understand about the names." I had a feeling there was a lot Blades had left out when discussing the Devil's Fury. I knew he worried about throwing too much at me at once.

"Since we're all family, you're welcome to call me Jameson when it's just us, or you can call me Dingo if that's preferable."

"Thank you for protecting my daughter," I said.

"She's amazing." Dingo smiled at her. "I'm lucky she agreed to be mine. She's both sweet and fierce. Perfect combination if you ask me."

I wasn't sure what to make of his words. Had there been a time since coming here that my daughter had needed to be fierce, as he'd called her? They made it sound like she'd been fine since coming to the Devil's Fury. Had there been an incident or something? I wanted to ask and yet didn't feel like I had the right to pry. I was seeing my daughter again for the first time in so very long. In a lot of ways, we were strangers.

"So, what did you do to the place that was holding Mom hostage?" Meiling asked, glancing over at her dad. "I hope you made them all suffer."

I gaped at my daughter. I'd never counted on her being so bloodthirsty. Perhaps I should have. She was Blades' daughter as well, after all. It made sense she'd be every bit as fierce as he was. Now I understood the comment Dingo made.

"I killed all the men, freed the women, and set the building on fire," Blades said. "Then I knocked a man unconscious in a diner for talking shit about your mom."

Meiling nodded. "Good. They deserved whatever they got."

"I hope it's okay, but I ordered food," Dingo said. "Pizza and pasta. I wasn't sure what China liked so I tried to get a variety. Got some of those garlic knots too, since your daughter is addicted to them."

Meiling elbowed him in the ribs, and he grunted even though I knew she couldn't have hit him hard enough for it to hurt. He winked at her, and she narrowed her eyes. Still, I could see the love and affection they shared and knew she wasn't truly cross with him. It seemed she had a sassy side. I smiled a little as I observed them.

"She's not big on pizza, but she'll eat it," Blades said. "Or at least, she used to. We've mostly been cooking at home. In fact, she was mad at me for not telling her you were coming over in enough time for her to make something. I was honestly afraid if I gave her too much warning, she'd find a way to get out of it."

"I'm just glad I finally get to see you," Meiling said, hugging me again. "But I understand. When I first came here, I felt so out of place."

"I thought..." I swallowed hard. "I thought you might be ashamed of me."

Tears slipped down my daughter's cheeks. "Mom, I could never feel ashamed of you. I love you. The moment I found out you were alive and you'd been kidnapped, all I could think about was finding you and bringing you home. I'm so glad you're here."

Blades put his arm around my shoulders. "We both are. She's every bit as beautiful as she was the last time I saw her. I only wish I could track down every man who's ever dared lay a hand on her and end their fucking lives. Miserable bastards need to be sent to hell."

Dingo nodded. "On the express train."

I couldn't help but laugh. It bubbled up inside me and spilled past my lips, surprising not only me but everyone else in the room. Blades pulled me tighter against his side. I didn't know why I found their words so funny. Or maybe I'd finally cracked after all the stress since Blades found me. Although, I could admit it was all self-induced. He'd done everything in his power to set me at ease. It was my own thoughts and worries that were driving me crazy.

"Have you left the compound yet?" Meiling asked.

"No. Your father has ordered stuff and had someone deliver it to the house," I said. I reached up to touch the scars on my face.

"Do they bother you that much?" she asked. "The scars, I mean."

"People will stare and whisper," I said.

"Not if we cover them up." Meiling took my hand. "Let me run home and grab my makeup. I don't usually wear a bunch of it, but I do have the stuff we'd need. Jameson likes for me to be prepared, so I have a little of everything even if I mostly wear a tinted lip balm."

"What are you trying to ask her, Mei?" Dingo tugged on her hair. "I think you need to be clearer about what you want."

"Oh." Her eyes widened. "Sorry, Mom. I thought we could all go to the mall or something. I'm sure you took me with you shopping before, even though I was too small to remember. I thought it would be a fun experience for us to share."

Shopping with my daughter? I knew it was a common thing that most parents had done with their children. The thought of being around so many people made my throat feel tight, but I knew I needed to leave the house at some point.

"All right. I'll try, but…"

Blades kissed the top of my head. "If it's too much after we've been there long enough for you to go into one store with our daughter, then I'll bring you home."

I hesitated a moment, but knew I'd give in. How could I tell the man no? The doorbell rang and Meiling went to answer, calling out to Dingo a moment later. They returned to the kitchen with the boxes of pizza and pasta containers. Blades pulled out a chair for me, making me sit even though he knew damn well I was about to get out plates and such. Instead, he gathered everything, then sat down so we could eat.

Meiling did her best to engage me in conversation as we ate. I responded as best I could, but sometimes all I could do was whisper a one-word answer. I knew she wanted more, but this was harder for me than anyone realized. Blades was right about me not hiding in this house anymore. I knew it, but it didn't mean it would be easy to venture out in the world.

After everyone finished, Dingo helped Blades clear the table and Meiling stood. She looked like she was ready to dash out the door, and I figured she was going to get the makeup she'd mentioned. She'd probably want to talk more while she covered up my scars. So far, she hadn't asked the one thing I'd dreaded most -- what had happened to me. She skirted around the topic, even though I could tell she wanted to ask.

"There's something I need to do if we're heading out. How long will it take the two of you to get ready?" Blades asked.

Meiling pressed her lips together and tipped her head to the side, studying me. "Hmm. Maybe an hour? I need to get my stuff from the house, and I thought I might style Mom's hair."

"I'll make it work," he said.

What was he up to now? I waited for Meiling and Dingo to leave before I turned to ask him, only to find him with his phone to his ear. He grinned at me, and I had a feeling he was about to do something ridiculous.

"Hey, Outlaw. I have a favor. You can use the money from my account, but I want either an SUV or truck in my driveway within the hour with the title in my name. I don't care how fancy it is as long as it's new with a warranty."

I didn't hear what the other man said, but it seemed to be favorable since Blades thanked him and hung up. I stared at him, wondering if he'd lost his mind.

"You're just going to buy a car sight unseen? Do you even know what that will cost?"

He snorted. "Do you?"

He had a good point. No, I didn't. It wasn't like I'd been able to leave the brothel. The last time I'd bought something that big and expensive I'd been in college, and technically my parents had paid for it. But I knew how much they'd cost back then, and I was certain it was double or triple those amounts now.

"I'm not broke, China. *We* aren't. My money is yours to use. In fact, once you're more comfortable going out, we'll stop by the bank and have you added to the account."

"I don't need all that."

He shook his head and sighed. "Yeah, sweetheart. You do. How else are you going to shop with our daughter, go to lunch, or buy groceries without having me with you? I want you to become independent. Not saying it has to happen right away, but some day you'll be ready. I want everything in place when that time comes."

"So the vehicle is really for me?" I asked.

"Yeah. I'll drive us around for now, until you tell me you're ready to give it a shot. I'm guessing you haven't been behind the wheel of a car in a long-ass time."

He was right. I hadn't. The thought of driving again made me apprehensive. What if I didn't remember all the rules? What if I caused an accident?

He kissed my forehead. "Stop worrying, China. Everything will be fine."

It was easy for him to say! It didn't take long before Meiling returned with Dingo. She came in carrying a tote bag, and I wondered exactly how much makeup she planned to slather on my face. I led the way to the master bathroom and sat on a stool that was usually shoved under the counter.

"Ready, Mom?" she asked.

"If I say no, does that mean we get to stay home?" She smiled, although I noticed it didn't reach her eyes. I felt horrible and wished I could recall the words. She wanted to spend time with me, and I was still trying to hide from the world. "I'm sorry. Go ahead, Meiling."

I closed my eyes and waited patiently as she covered my scars, smoothed out my skin tone, then added blush, mascara, and some lipstick. I had to admit I looked nice when she finished, and I couldn't see any of my scars unless I leaned in really close to the mirror. Anyone standing a respectable distance from me wouldn't be able to tell I had them.

"Thank you, my daughter. You did a wonderful job."

She smiled widely and hugged me. I noticed she lingered a moment, and I wondered how much she'd suffered all these years without me. Not only because of what happened but simply because she'd needed her parents.

"Let me do your hair and we'll be finished." She combed it out, braided a few sections, then twisted them into a knot. Using decorative combs she found in a drawer, she secured it in place. "Let's go buy you some new clothes and anything else you need or want. I have a feeling Dad is going to let you buy anything you want."

I huffed. "The crazy man just bought a car. I think he's spent enough already."

She snickered. "Trust me, that's only going to be the beginning. If he's anything like Dingo, be prepared for him to drop thousands more on you over the next month or two. You might be able to get him to slow down after that, but don't count on it."

"How does he have so much money if he's been locked up?" I asked.

She shrugged. "Not entirely sure, but I bet the club has been taking care of him. Even if he was in prison, he was still a patched member. If I understand it all correctly, that means he got a percentage of the monthly profits even if he didn't do the actual work. Just not as large a cut as anyone actively earning money for the Devil's Fury."

"All these years?" I asked.

"Well, no. I don't think so. But definitely since Grizzly took over as President. He's a great guy. A little scary-looking at first, and he comes across as gruff. You'll like him once you adjust."

I hoped she was right. If I didn't like being here, I knew Blades would either find a way to keep me by his side, or he'd walk out the gates with me. Would the club really let him do something like that? I didn't think so. For his sake, and Meiling's, I needed to make this work.

"One foot in front of the other," I mumbled.

Meiling giggled a little. "Isn't that from a kid's Christmas movie?"

I blinked. "Um. Is it?"

"I think it's part of a song or something, but it's also a saying… just to put one foot in front of the other. I think that's the right attitude, Mom. Stop trying to look at the bigger picture and focus on right now. Not even today, but this very minute or maybe the next. Trust me. It will lessen your anxiety."

"My Meiling is so smart." I reached out to lightly touch her cheek. "I'm honored to have you as my daughter."

She gave me a tight smile and I saw her eyes were glassy with unshed tears. It seemed I kept making her want to cry. I'd do my best to have a nice time with her today, and make sure she smiled. If anyone deserved to be happy, it was her.

"Love you, Mom," she whispered.

"I love you too."

She held my hand as we went to find Blades and Dingo, then everyone loaded into the new SUV sitting in the driveway. I had no idea how he'd managed to procure one so fast, but it looked nice. I hoped Meiling was wrong about the amount of money he'd spend on me. The man was going to drain the account at this rate. I much preferred having groceries over things I didn't need. Maybe we needed to have a talk later today.

Chapter Five

Blades

The mall was the one place I hated with a passion, but for my girls, I'd gladly endure it. Especially if it gave Meiling and China time together. I knew my woman wouldn't feel safe venturing out without protection, and since she'd just met Dingo, that meant I had to tag along. Honestly, I didn't mind. While this wasn't on my top one hundred favorite places to be, I enjoyed watching the various expressions on China's face.

So far, our daughter had talked her into three outfits and a new pair of shoes. Little she did realize, I was paying attention to every little thing she admired. I could tell which ones she really wanted, and those she only found mildly interesting. She hadn't caught on to the fact I'd called a Prospect to follow along behind us. I gave him a subtle signal for each item I wanted to buy for her, then he'd get it as we were leaving the store. Of course, it meant he had to make multiple trips to the vehicle so China wouldn't wonder why we had so many bags.

She lightly ran her fingers over a purple leather purse. It was on the small side, but since she didn't really have much to put it in right now, it would be just about right for her. I noticed there was a matching wallet on the shelf above it. Meiling glanced from her mom to me, flashed me a smile, then hustled China to the next shop. I shook my head, knowing I'd been caught by at least one of my girls. I pointed to both items and the Prospect gave me a thumbs-up before snatching them and heading for the register.

Dingo leaned in and dropped his voice low enough no one else would hear. "She's going to be pissed when she gets in the car and sees all the crap you've been buying."

"That's why I told Van to bring one of the club trucks instead of riding his bike. If China comments about it, I can tell her I thought we might need a backup vehicle in case Meiling wasn't ready to leave at the same time as us."

He shook his head. "All right. I still say this isn't going to go over very well for you."

"I'll give her the things she needs now. Other stuff I'll hide somewhere and give her as random gifts or set a few aside for her birthday or Christmas."

"I didn't think about it, but you said China wasn't born in the US. Does she celebrate Christmas? Meiling doesn't know much about her heritage," Dingo said.

"Yes and no. For me, she put up a tree, hung stockings for us, and we celebrated like other families by opening presents and having a nice meal together. But in her home country, the Lunar New Year is a family celebration. China once told me they still enjoy shopping and looking at decorations during Christmas in her hometown, but it's nothing like what we do here."

He nodded. "I'll have to read up on it. I'm sure Meiling would like to celebrate the Lunar New Year with her mom. I want to make sure she gets to experience all the things she's missed."

"Same." I was surprised China had lasted as long as she had today. I noticed the way her gaze darted around whenever someone walked a little close to her, or if another shopper bumped into her. She hadn't panicked yet, and for that I was grateful. "I have a feeling we'll need to leave soon. She looks like she's wearing down."

"Want me to wrangle Mei? You know she can shop all day if I let her," Dingo said. "Although, it took me a while to convince her it was all right to spend my money."

I understood completely. With China, it would probably take me months, if not longer, to show her whatever I had belonged to her as well. I'd meant it when I said it wasn't *my* money in the bank but *our* money.

Dingo stepped closer to Meiling and whispered in her ear. I saw the way she eyed her mom and knew she saw the exhaustion on China's face as well, despite the fact she kept smiling at us. Now that we'd gotten her out of the house, I could tell she didn't want to disappoint Meiling by returning too soon. Stubborn woman! I'd told her we could leave whenever she wanted.

She paused and glanced at me over her shoulder. I held out a hand to her, and she came to me, pressing her face against my chest. I wrapped her in my arms and knew she was done for the day. I could feel the slight tremor running through her body.

"You did so good, China. I'm proud of you," I murmured.

"I don't think she's ready to leave," she said.

"Our daughter can return another day. Besides, Dingo would probably appreciate a reprieve from her emptying his account. Let's head back to the house. You can take a hot shower and put on something more comfortable."

"Time to go?" Meiling asked.

"Yeah. Let's call it a day. I think your mom needs some rest."

Disappointment flashed in her eyes, and I knew she'd wanted to come back to our house and visit a while longer. As much as I didn't want to run her off, I needed to think of what was best for China right now. She still had a lot of healing to do, but this had been an amazing first step.

"All right," Meiling said. "Can we all have dinner together tomorrow? I have some news I haven't shared with her yet."

I knew exactly what she wanted to tell her. Our daughter was expecting her first child, and while I was thrilled to be a grandpa sometime soon, I didn't know how China would react. I met Dingo's gaze and he seemed to understand my concerns.

"Let's save that for a little later," I whispered to Meiling. "I think she'll appreciate it more when she's had more time to adjust to her new life."

"Is something wrong?" China asked.

"No, sweetheart. Just don't want our daughter to overwhelm you."

Meiling sighed. "Fine. But can we still come over for dinner tomorrow? Or maybe you could come to our house?"

Dingo shook his head. Yeah, that wasn't going to happen. They'd already started putting a nursery together. I didn't need China seeing it anytime soon. Not until she'd been told about the baby.

"Your mom would probably feel more comfortable staying at her house tomorrow," he said gently, trying not to upset his wife. "I'm sure she'll come see the house sometime soon. Give her more time, Mei. You're trying to rush things."

"All right. I won't be so pushy," she grumbled.

"I'll call you in the morning about dinner. If your mom isn't ready for more company that soon, we'll try the night after that."

Meiling placed her hands on her hips. "I'm not

company, Dad. I'm your daughter."

"I know, Meiling," I said softly. "I get it. I understand you want to spend as much time with your mom as you can, but please consider everything she's thinking and feeling right now."

Meiling gave me a nod, and we all made our way out of the mall and to the SUV. Van waved to me as he got into the truck, and as I opened the back hatch of my new ride to place the last few purchases into the vehicle, I noticed he'd already put most of our bags into the truck he was driving. He'd wait until I got home with China, went inside, and then he'd leave everything on the porch. While she showered, I'd hide the things I wasn't going to give her right away.

By the time we reached the house, I could tell China would be going to bed after her shower. She looked ready to drop from exhaustion, although I had a feeling it was more emotional than physical. She'd had a big day, and I knew it had been asking a lot for her to leave the house, especially the first time she saw our daughter after so long.

Dingo ushered Meiling into their vehicle and transferred her bags over. Everything else, I hauled into the house and followed China to the bedroom. I set them down on the mattress, figuring I'd sort them in a few minutes.

"Let me start the shower for you," I said.

"I'm not completely helpless," she mumbled.

"I didn't say you were. Maybe I like taking care of you."

She gave me a tired smile and I went into the bathroom, setting out a fresh towel for her, then turning on the taps in the shower and adjusting the temperature. Once it was ready, I called her into the bathroom and left her to have some time to herself. I'd check on her shortly. I quickly sorted the new items I'd already brought into the house, and separated the clothes into dark and light colors so I could wash everything. I remembered the way she used to sniff the laundry after it had come out of the dryer. I'd always found it to be a cute habit.

I poked my head into the bathroom and saw her leaning her forehead against the wall as the water ran down her neck and back. "Everything all right?"

"Yeah. Do I need to get out?"

"No, sweetheart. You take your time. I'll come back in a bit and see if you need anything. Just relax. If you want to switch to the tub and soak for a while, let me know."

"This is fine."

I went to the front door and opened it. Van had already dropped off everything and I carried it inside. I made it as far as the living room before I made the decision on what she'd get today, and what I'd put away for later. Anything I'd use as a gift I hid in the spare room closet at the top. It wasn't the ideal hiding spot, but it was the best I had for right now. I'd have to come up with something better later.

I placed the purse and wallet on the bed, along with a key ring. Walking over to the dresser, I pulled out my spare key. Well, technically it wasn't a "spare" any longer and now belonged to China. Maybe this would help her realize how much she belonged here with me.

I heard the water shut off, then the rustle of the towel as she dried off. I hadn't thought to take pajamas into the bathroom for her. The fact she came out completely bare without even the towel wrapped around her, nearly had my jaw dropping. The woman could still shock the hell out of me and make me harder than a damn post. Even twenty years from now, she'd be the most beautiful woman I'd ever seen.

"Damn. How can you still be so sexy?" I asked.

Her cheeks flushed. "You're still a flirt after all these years."

"I'm out of practice. The men in prison weren't exactly my type." Although, there were men who didn't care as long as they were getting some. Not me. It was pussy or nothing. Okay. Not *nothing* but my hand wasn't the same as a warm, willing woman.

"I think you're still doing very well with it," she said. "Maybe too well."

I couldn't keep my gaze off her as she dressed in a cotton nightgown that went all the way to her knees. She'd chosen it because the gray material had been advertised as super soft, and the sleeves had a pretty floral print. Some men might prefer lingerie that was barely there. Not me. My China looked amazing in anything, and she had my cock's attention. Except I wouldn't be touching her tonight.

She came over and eyed the items on the bed. "What's all this?"

"I saw the way you looked at the purse at the mall, and I knew you were going to need one. Same for the wallet and key ring. I put the house key on there already, and we can add the SUV key fob to it tomorrow."

Her brow furrowed. "I noticed you didn't put a key in the ignition when you were driving. You pushed a button and it started. When did that become a thing?"

"Not sure. If one of my brothers didn't have a vehicle that started the same way, I'd have never figured out how to drive our new car." I turned on the TV hanging on the wall across from the bed, then tossed the remote onto the bed as I stripped out of my clothes.

I watched China from the corner of my eye as I pulled on a pair of sweats and a clean tee. She ran her fingers over the purse, then tucked the wallet and key ring inside before setting it on the dresser. After I dressed, I flipped the covers back and China climbed into bed. She scooted to the center, and I lay down beside her. Pulling the covers over the both of us, I curled my arm around China, then I did the one thing I knew would prove I loved her... I handed her the remote.

She smiled faintly and selected a movie before reaching across me to put the remote on the table. "You sure you won't regret this?"

"Sweetheart, I don't care what you put on. As long as you're happy, that's all that matters. I'd watch every sappy romance you can find on there, as long as it made you keep smiling. Because that's what I enjoy seeing. Doesn't matter to me what's on TV."

"You're too sweet," she murmured, snuggling closer and focusing on whatever she'd selected to watch. I knew she wouldn't last for the entire thing. And I'd been right. Within twenty minutes, she'd fallen asleep.

Having her here with me filled me with peace. I'd never thought to experience this again, and yet here we were. Now that I had her back, I was never letting her go. Even if she decided to never leave the house again, I'd be content knowing she was here waiting for me to return from whatever job I was on. I hadn't been assigned many tasks since I'd come back to the Devil's Fury. Something told me that would change before too long. I knew Grizzly was giving me time with Meiling, and to set right all the wrongs my family had experienced since I'd been locked up.

I reached out to snag my phone and quickly shot off a text to Outlaw.

Is there a way to track all the men who have hurt China since she was kidnapped?

I waited for his response. It took him a few minutes, but I finally got one. *That's like finding a needle in a haystack. No, we can't track everyone down, especially any paying with cash.*

Figured as much. Hadn't hurt to try. *Thanks anyway.*

Instead of getting revenge for her, I'd just have to make sure no one treated her poorly ever again. She was my goddess. The mother of my child. And the only woman I'd ever love. If anyone hurt her feelings, they'd answer to me. The next man who called her a whore wouldn't be walking away. He'd have to be carried out -- in a body bag.

Chapter Six
China

The day had finally come. I couldn't put it off any longer, even though I'd tried. It was time to meet the rest of the club. I'd been at the Devil's Fury for a little over two weeks now. I'd become more comfortable around Meiling and Dingo, and I was slowly starting to feel like we were a family. There was still a whispering voice in my mind claiming I wasn't good enough to be here. I did my best to ignore it, and most days I succeeded.

There was this nervous energy racing through me, and it felt like I had a knot in my stomach. Blades reminded me the only women in attendance today would be me, our daughter Meiling, and Adalia. I hadn't met her yet, but he'd told me about her. Adopted daughter of Grizzly, and old lady of someone named Badger.

I stared at the clubhouse and ran my palms up and down my denim-clad thighs. I'd worn a plain shirt and a pair of ankle boots. As I watched other people go past us and into the building, I realized I'd dressed appropriately. Good thing I'd listened to Blades and changed out of the leggings and tunic top I'd picked out at first. Although, it had been incredibly comfortable. Maybe I should have kept the outfit on.

"Ready?" he asked, holding out his hand to me.

I had to bite back my response. He didn't need me being sarcastic right now. I could tell how much this meant to him. Gripping his hand tighter than necessary, I followed him into the clubhouse. The laughter spilled through the open doors, and I tried not to think about how many people were inside.

"They won't bite," he said. "Let's head in and I'll

introduce you to everyone."

I nodded and we let the doors shut behind us. He cleared his throat and yelled out in a voice so loud I winced, "I need everyone's attention!"

The chatter died down until the room became silent. Now I felt even more uncomfortable. I could feel all of them staring at me. Meiling came over and took my other hand, then laid her head against my shoulder.

"It's okay, Mom. They're all going to love you," she whispered.

"You all know I left about two weeks ago to get China. She's been struggling a bit and trying to acclimate to living here. I only ask you don't all rush her at once. She's always been on the shy side." He looked down at me and winked, with a smile on his face. Yes, I was, and right now he was embarrassing the hell out of me. Damn man probably knew it too. Although, I did appreciate his words of caution to everyone in the room.

I'd never done well around strangers. If he hadn't stepped in to help me all those years ago, I never would have had the courage to talk to him. He'd seemed so wild, and too much older than me to be interested in a college girl. When I found out how wrong I was, I'd never been more grateful. Blades was the best thing that ever happened to me. Well, him and Meiling.

Dingo stepped closer. "There's one more bit of news. Something Meiling and I want to share. Most of you already know, but we're making an official announcement. We're going to have a baby!"

I tensed and stared at my daughter. "You're pregnant?"

Why hadn't she told me sooner? The way Blades

tightened his hold on me was enough to say it was his doing. Had he worried I wouldn't be able to handle it? I could say I'd have preferred to find out in a different setting. It felt like I'd been ambushed.

She nodded, her eyes shining with happiness. "I'm terrified and excited. With everything that happened and the hell I went through in the foster system, I'm worried I won't know how to be a mom. At the same time, I can't wait to meet the little person growing inside me."

I'd finally adjusted to being a mother again and being with Blades. Now I was going to be a grandmother? I was right there with her on the worrying part. I'd failed her as a child. What if I was horrible at being a grandparent?

Meiling squeezed my arm. "It's fine, Mom. We can figure this out together."

"You're right." I kissed her cheek. "I'm happy for the two of you."

Blades put his arm around my shoulders. "Come on. I'm going to introduce you to a few people, then I'll find a spot for you to sit and get you a plate of food and something to drink."

He led me over to an older man standing next to a couple. I didn't even have to read their cuts to know they must be Grizzly, Badger, and Adalia.

"Welcome to the Devil's Fury, China," Grizzly said, reaching out to shake my hand. "This is my daughter, Adalia, and my son-in-law, Badger. You need anything and can't find Blades, Dingo, or Meiling, then you come find one of us. We'll be happy to help in any way we can."

His hand was warm and despite his rough appearance, I could tell he was a kind man. "Thank you."

He rocked back on his heels and sighed. "Wish my May were here to see this. The club is growing, and we're going to have kids running around before too long."

The way he spoke of her, I assumed her to be dead. Adalia's eyes darkened a moment, but she quickly put a smile on her face and leaned in to give me a quick hug.

"What Dad said... I'm glad you're here, and I know Mei is too." She elbowed Badger. "It's about time we had more women to help even out the massive amount of testosterone in this place."

"So before Dingo married my daughter, you were the only woman here?" I asked.

She nodded. "Yeah, after Mom died anyway. I still miss her every single day. Mei is so lucky to have you in her life again."

She was right. It was a miracle Blades had found me, and that we'd both been reunited with our daughter. He led me over to a table, stopping along the way to introduce me to Outlaw, Wolf, and Colorado. There were still quite a few people I hadn't met, but I was starting to feel a little overwhelmed. Being around so many men made me feel like I was back in the Silk Purse.

"Wait here and I'll bring you something," Blades said.

Meiling and Dingo came to sit with us, and I noticed Adalia, Grizzly, and Badger claimed the next table. It was almost as if they were trying to surround me. If they were, then I really owed them. I wasn't sure I'd ever adjust to being around so many people again, much less men.

"Mom, everyone knows your story," Meiling said. "They're not going to hurt you, and none of them think badly about you. You survived, and that's all that matters."

"I know you're right. It doesn't stop me from feeling dirty or unworthy of being here," I said. "It's not something that will go away quickly, but I promise to try and get to know the people here."

"Does this mean you're ready to go out and do more things with me?" she asked. "Like maybe help me shop for the baby?"

I reached over to take her hand. "Yes. I'm sorry I haven't been a good mom to you. I've felt so incredibly lost. There are things about your father that are both familiar and different from when I knew him before. It's been difficult to figure out where I fit in, and whether or not we can truly pick up where we left off."

Blades returned and set a plate in front of me with a few finger foods, as well as a soda. I nibbled on the food, knowing he'd fuss if I didn't eat something. Someone started some music, which seemed to come from speakers in the corners of the room. I wondered how loud this place would be during a wild party. Not that I wanted to attend one.

"So this is your first time here?" Adalia asked, angling her chair toward me. "But you were with Blades before?"

"The club wasn't the same back then," Blades said. "Different President. Different rules. China and Meiling wouldn't have been safe here."

"I'm the one who started to change things," Grizzly said. "When I fell in love with May. I knew I couldn't walk away from the club, but I wanted to spend as much time with her as possible. After I took over, I made even more changes."

"Is there anyone else still in the club from back then?" Adalia asked.

"King went to prison and died inside," Blades said. "I'm not sure what happened to all the others."

"They're all dead," Grizzly said. "Except for one other. Yeti. He went Nomad. I've seen him now and then. Tried to get him to settle here, but he hasn't yet."

"That's so sad," Adalia said. "It must have been so hard to come back to the club and find everything had changed so drastically, and other than my dad, you didn't know anyone here."

"It was," Blades said. "But I have my daughter and China. Nothing else matters. Not to mention I can actually live with them here at the compound and don't have to hide them anymore. I don't mind the changes. Grizzly has done a great job with this place."

"You can thank May," Grizzly said. "She made me want to be a better man."

"The two of you technically have some in-laws," Dingo said. "My sister is the old lady to the Sergeant-at-Arms over at the Devil's Boneyard. Jordan and Havoc. I'd like to invite them here for a visit when Meiling and China are ready to meet them."

Grizzly chuckled and shook his head. "Not sure anyone is ever ready for your sister. I've heard some wild stories from Scratch and Cinder."

"She's not exactly tame," Dingo said. "She had to be strong to survive."

"What happened?" I asked. "Or is that too personal?"

"You're family, China, and I know Jordan wouldn't care if I told you. She went to prison for assault. Met Havoc the day she got out because our brother fucked up. He didn't go get her and she tried to walk to town. Passed out on the side of the road."

"You didn't mention a brother before," Blades said.

"He's dead. Good fucking riddance! He did his best to kill Jordan because he was jealous of how quickly she was accepted by the club. He'd only been a Prospect at the time and felt like they owed it to him to patch him in." Dingo leaned back in his chair. "He was too fucking stupid to keep breathing."

I was starting to get the idea that Blades' reaction to finding me in the Silk Purse was just another day to these people. Meiling had suffered horribly and been accepted by them. Dingo said his sister went to prison for assault. I wondered if Adalia had a similar story, but I didn't feel right asking.

"Is there anything you need?" Adalia asked. "I'm sure Blades has bought you everything you could possibly think of, but sometimes people need more than material things."

"I'm fine but thank you. Are you and my daughter close?" I asked.

"Not as much as I'd like to be," Adalia said. "Meiling is still a bit new here. I think we get along well, though. I'd love to visit with the two of you sometime. Maybe have a girls' day either here at the compound or out at a café or something."

"That sounds nice, doesn't it, Mom?" Meiling asked.

This was what my daughter needed, and most likely I did too. A friend. Someone other than Blades and our daughter who could listen if I decided I needed to talk, or just didn't want to feel quite so alone.

"Do you like green tea?" I asked.

"I enjoy it sometimes. I tend to prefer fruit-flavored teas, but as long as it's hot, I drink just about all of them," Adalia said.

Blades had come home the other day with a

Chinese tea table. He'd set it up in one of the spare rooms, and I hadn't had a chance to use it yet. I knew it had to be an antique. Hand-carved with inlaid mother of pearl and a glass top, with six stools that tucked under it. The one he'd bought looked similar to the one my parents had when I was younger.

"Do you want to invite them over?" Blades asked, leaning in closer so only I could hear him.

"You wouldn't mind?" I asked.

He shook his head. "Go ahead. In fact, the three of you could go to the house now, and I'll stay here with my brothers. It will be nice to have a low-key party."

Badger snorted. "I bet within an hour or less of the women vacating the building, someone will call in the club pussy."

Adalia smacked him on the thigh. "Don't say stuff like that in front of China! She may not know about that part of the club yet. You're going to scare her off."

Blades groaned and ran a hand down his face. "There are women who like to come here and party. And by that I mean they enjoy sex with any biker who will have them whether it's for fifteen minutes or the entire night. Most are hoping they'll get claimed, but a lot of them just want to take a walk on the wild side. If they show up, I'm leaving."

"Same," Dingo said. "If you want, you can come hang out at the house while the women are over at your place. I have cold beer in the fridge. Badger and Grizzly are welcome too."

"You said this party was to welcome me," I said. "Won't everyone be angry if I leave so soon?"

Grizzly stood up and yelled for everyone to shut the hell up. "The women are going to go bond in a quieter environment. Try not to tear the place up in their absence. If you let the club whores in, you'd better make damn sure they don't wander and cross paths with Adalia, Meiling, or China. Am I understood?"

"Don't worry, Pres. We don't need the women to have some fun," a man shouted back.

"Yeah, we'll see how long it takes for you to change your mind," Grizzly said.

I stood when Meiling and Adalia did and followed them outside with the men right behind us. Grizzly gave Adalia a set of keys.

"Take them with you. Badger and I are close enough to our homes we can get our bikes and ride over to Dingo's place. Just drop it back off at my house when you're done," Grizzly said. He turned to me with a smile. "China, it was really nice meeting you, and I hope we'll see more of you around here. Make sure someone points out my house so you can find me easily if you ever need something."

Before I could say anything, Meiling was ushering me over to the vehicle and opening a door for me. I climbed inside and placed my hand against the window. Blades pressed his to the other side of the glass. It was my first time going anywhere without him since he'd found me. He'd run some errands and gone out on a job or two, but I'd stayed home those days.

Adalia drove to my house and pulled into the driveway. Meiling beat me out of the car and opened my door again. I shook my head at her. "Are you trying to be a proper gentleman?"

"Not hardly. Just showing my mother some respect."

I lightly touched her cheek. "Such a good girl."

I led everyone inside and showed them the room

with the tea table. While Meiling and Adalia admired it, I went to make the tea. If only I had a proper Chinese tea set, then this would be perfect. Having people in the house didn't make me as anxious as it had before. Inviting them over had been the right thing to do. It was one more step toward leading a normal life again.

Chapter Seven

Blades

I heard voices in the kitchen and picked up my phone to check the time. How the hell had I slept so late? I glanced over to China's side of the bed and placed my hand on her pillow. Ice cold. She must have been up for a while. I didn't know why she hadn't woken me.

She'd been back in my life a little over a month now. I'd watched her slowly become more like the woman I used to know, and less afraid of everything around her. She still had her moments where doubts would creep in, but she'd gotten better about shaking them off. While I knew my love for her played a part, I couldn't take all the credit. She'd bonded with Meiling and Dingo, and even Adalia stopped by more frequently these days.

I sighed and rubbed a hand over my face. Listening intently, I tried to figure out who had come over. It sounded like Meiling, but I heard male voices too. More than one. What the hell was so important it couldn't have waited until after lunch?

Getting out of bed, I went to the bathroom, brushed my teeth, then put on a shirt. Whoever was here would have to deal with the fact I was wearing sweatpants. They'd infiltrated my house before I'd had a chance to wake up. If they'd wanted to see me showered and fully dressed, then they should have fucking waited.

"What's all the noise?" I asked, stepping into the kitchen. I froze when I saw Grizzly, Badger, Outlaw, Meiling, and my beautiful China. Why the hell was the Pres here? "I hope there's coffee. I feel like whatever conversation is about to happen will require a few cups."

Badger smirked. Yeah. That alone told me I might need an entire pot. What the hell happened while I was asleep? I eyed China to see how she was doing. She calmly sat at the table with Meiling next to her, both sipping some tea. The coffee pot on the counter was already full, which meant she'd been prepared for me to wake up and need caffeine. I poured a cup and stood behind China, placing one hand on her shoulder.

"All right. Someone start talking." I took a swallow, then another, wondering if it would be bad for me to drain the entire cup in one go.

"We actually came bearing gifts," Outlaw said. "Except China doesn't want it."

"What sort of gift is she turning down?" I asked.

"The money from the Silk Purse," Meiling said. "Outlaw drained their accounts and put everything into one only he can access for right now. Mom doesn't want the money."

I could understand her reasoning. Although, she hadn't been the only one to suffer. "What about the others? Did you offer them anything? I'm sure they could use some cash to help restart their lives."

"I did," Outlaw said. "They each accepted five thousand so they could get a place of their own and buy necessities. Then I sent another five thousand per woman to the people helping them, in case they run out before they find jobs."

"Dad, there's over half a million left," Meiling said.

I let out a low whistle. That was a big chunk of money. And that was only from the Silk Purse? I didn't see how the place had made so much without spending it elsewhere. Something seemed off. I eyed

Outlaw, but he gave me a blank expression. Yeah, he'd found funds elsewhere, which meant he'd probably drained the accounts of every person involved, or as many as he and his hacker friends had been able to track. There was a chance that half a million would continue to grow as they found more of the bastards.

"So, what do you want them to do with it, China? It's dirty money. We all get that, and I understand how it might make you feel to accept it. However, think of it as combat pay."

"Really, Dad?" Meiling rolled her eyes. "That's the best you could come up with?"

I swallowed more coffee and tried to think of a solution. Something told me these men weren't leaving until China either took the money or told them what to do with it. She was a kind and giving woman, one who didn't like to see other people hurt.

"What if we donate some?" I asked. "Women's shelters, organizations fighting human trafficking, orphanages... all those places would love to have some money coming in." I squeezed China's shoulder. "Maybe we could put fifty thousand into an account for our grandchild. They could use it to help pay for college later, or anything else they might need."

China sighed. "Half a million is a lot of money. I don't feel right accepting more than the others did."

"Ma'am, I don't mean to be offensive, but you were in that shithole a lot longer than those other women," Badger said. "You lost nearly two decades of your life, not to mention missing out on watching Mei grow up and being able to keep her safe. Those other women hadn't been there more than a few weeks to a few years."

"It's your call, China," I said. "But I think it would be a mistake to not accept any of it. Badger is right. Those people owe you so much more than a half million dollars could ever buy. You can't get all those years back."

"I want at least half to be donated to charities," she said.

"Not a problem," Outlaw said. "I'll compile a list of options and we can go over them later. I'll let you select the places that receive the money and how much to each one."

"And the rest, Mom?" Meiling asked.

Grizzly cleared his throat. "I actually came for a different reason, so hold off on answering for a moment. I realize you've holed up in this house quite a bit since returning, and it's given you and Blades time to bond again. But being in the compound has its disadvantages, like people dropping in."

"Glad you noticed," I muttered. He narrowed his eyes at me, and I smiled into my coffee cup as I finished it off. While I poured another, I listened to what he had to say.

"Badger and Adalia helped me put something together for the two of you. We've booked you an Airbnb in New Orleans. It's an apartment in the French Quarter, but it's a secure location. There's a code to access the courtyard and another to get into the apartment. We booked it for a full week." Grizzly pulled out a chair and sat. "You could use some of the money to enjoy your time there. Go sightseeing, buy souvenirs, shop at places we don't have around here. Maybe go on one of those haunted tours or something."

"New Orleans?" I asked. "What made you pick that place?"

"One of the times Adalia met with China and Meiling, they talked about places they'd never been.

China said she hadn't been to New Orleans, Disney World, and a bunch of other places. New Orleans was the closest, and I honestly can't see you at Disney World," Badger said. "Not unless you booked the entire park because you'd probably scare the shit out of all the kids."

"Real funny, asshole," I muttered. "China, would you like to spend a week with me in New Orleans?"

She glanced up at me. "Is it really all right?"

"Of course. I don't have anything lined up around here, and Grizzly wouldn't have booked the place if he planned to send me on a job. You haven't decided if you want to work or just stay home, and like I told you before, I'm perfectly happy with you being here every day. You've earned a few decades to relax."

"I think you'd have fun, Mom," Meiling said.

"When would we have to leave?" I asked.

"You can check in as early as this afternoon. I explained to the owners that this was a gift so I wasn't sure how quickly you'd be able to get there. I'll provide you with everything they sent me, as well as their name and number. They're a really nice couple. They said if you needed anything, let them know." Grizzly stood and pushed in his chair. "Also, don't forget there's a club down there. I already ran this past the Broken Bastards, so they're aware you'll be vacationing. It's not an issue for you to wear your cut. That being said… if you'd like to take it and not necessarily wear it the entire time, I'm fine with that. I know people can give us pointed looks."

"It's roughly a six-hour drive, right?" I asked.

"Probably closer to five," Badger said. "If you speed for part of the trip, then even less."

"Thanks. We appreciate the trip and the thought you put into it. Now, China… tell Outlaw how much you want transferred to our account for the trip," I said.

"I don't know what things cost," she said.

"What if I put a few thousand into Blades' account, then open one just for you? On your way out of town, you could stop at a branch in a bigger city. They'd be able to print off a debit card for you within a few minutes. I'll print off anything you need and leave it at the front gate for you. The rest we can sort out later," Outlaw said.

"Sounds like a solid plan. Meiling, why don't you help your mother figure out what to pack? Check the weather forecast for that area during the days we'll be there. I'd imagine it will be hotter there since it's farther south."

Meiling and China left the room, and I could hear the two of them talking about the trip. I was happy to see China excited about something.

"Thank you for making this club what it is today," I said. "The old Devil's Fury would have never done anything like this, and I don't just mean the trip. They'd have kept the money and used it to expand the gun and drug business. I'm proud to call the three of you my brothers."

"We're glad you're back," Grizzly said. "Sorry it took so long to realize you'd been set up. Never thought to go talk to you and ask. I should have known the old officers would do something underhanded and hang a brother out to dry."

"We'll head out so you can get on the road soon." Each one shook my hand before leaving the house.

I found Meiling and China in the bedroom with a mountain of clothes on the mattress. I'd been expanding her wardrobe a few pieces at a time, and sometimes sneaking in handfuls of things, then pretending I had no clue where they came from. I knew I hadn't fooled her. It wasn't like there was a clothing fairy who dropped by after she went to bed.

"I think that's a little much for a week away," I said.

"She doesn't know what she'll want to wear," Meiling said.

"Then pick five outfits and we'll buy some more after we get there. Just make sure you have comfortable shoes. I've heard parking is a bitch down there, so people walk to a lot of places."

"Since when did you research New Orleans?" Meiling asked.

"Well, I haven't recently. Met some people from there a long time ago. They said they lived in the French Quarter and the only time they drove was when they went to other areas. Otherwise, they walked everywhere. It could have changed since then, but better safe than sorry."

"Give me twenty minutes and I'll have Mom all packed," Meiling said.

I went to the spare room and dug through the items I'd still kept hidden from China. One of them had been a small suitcase. Even though I hadn't had plans to travel at the time, I knew there was always a chance we'd go somewhere. Besides, it had been on sale and was the same color as the purple purse I'd bought for her. I took it to the bedroom and set it on the floor beside the bed. China eyed it, then me but didn't say a word. Looked like she'd finally figured out things would keep randomly appearing.

"I'll be packed and out of your way within a few minutes." I reached into the top of the closet and took down a duffle, then rolled and packed some jeans, tees, socks, and underwear. I grabbed two new toothbrushes and an unopened toothpaste, making sure Meiling knew I'd already packed them. It was one less thing for China to worry about. Then I shoved my deodorant, brush, and cologne into the bag.

"I'll be in the kitchen," I said.

Exactly twenty minutes later, they joined me, with China rolling her suitcase behind her. Looked like the fun part started now… the long-ass fucking drive.

We loaded our bags into the SUV and hugged Meiling goodbye. I stopped at the front gate to get the papers Outlaw said he'd leave and found a note with the bank location for China's debit card. While I might be behind the times as far as technology went, Meiling had shown me a few things. Including how to use the maps app. I loaded the address of the bank, then pulled through the gates.

"The bank he picked is about two hours away. If you want, we can stop for lunch while we're there," I said.

"Why didn't you say something?" she asked. "I was so wrapped up in everything going on I never made you breakfast."

"China, I'm a grown-ass man. While I appreciate you cooking, I'm capable of feeding myself. The better question is whether or not *you* ate before I woke up."

She didn't comment, which told me plenty. It looked like I'd be stopping before the bank, and we'd have lunch later in the day. Once we made it out of town, I kept an eye out for restaurant signs. I wasn't about to let the stubborn woman go hungry for two hours.

She reached over and placed her hand on my thigh. Shifting in my seat, I did my best to keep my cock from going rock hard. I hoped the place in New

Orleans had a decent bed because the only plan I had for my woman tonight was hearing her scream my name. Well, maybe not scream it. In a place like New Orleans, they might think I was killing her. Shit. Why did it have to be an apartment?

Chapter Eight
China

The apartment was really a studio, but it was clean, and the furniture looked new. A queen bed took up the far wall, and they'd placed a love seat in the center of the back wall. A TV was mounted near the French doors. On the wall backing up to the bathroom, there was a two-burner cooktop, a small fridge, and a microwave. They also had a round table with two chairs.

It was pretty perfect for a quick getaway for vacation. Blades had already told me we'd eat out for every meal. He wanted to visit Café Du Monde for some chicory coffee. I didn't know what a beignet was, but it sounded interesting. We were going there for breakfast in the morning. He'd also looked up several other places, and we'd found a folder of suggestions the apartment owners had left for us, including tours and must-see places.

"Not someplace I'd want to live full-time," Blades said. "But it's nice for the week."

"It feels authentic," I said. "It's older, much like the city. I think that's what I like about it. They could have modernized it more, but it would have taken away from the charm."

"Yeah, old like me," he said.

I smacked the back of my hand against his abdomen. "Hush! You think I didn't notice those younger women checking you out when we got here?"

"I didn't see them. Then again, the only woman I ever notice is you." He leaned down to kiss me, his lips lingering on mine for a moment. "I already have the most beautiful woman in the world. Why would I need anyone else?"

I could feel my cheeks warm and knew they had to be red. "Always a flirt. Do you even know how to *not* be one?"

"Probably not. At least, not when it comes to you. Anyone else I don't give a shit. They're lucky if I speak to them."

I knew he wasn't wrong. He really didn't like it when people came up to him and started talking. Even with his brothers, I noticed he sometimes glowered. He'd placed our bags at the foot of the bed and I went to unpack our bathroom things. After I set them on the sink and the edge of the tub, I went over to the folder and flipped through some of the restaurant options.

"Since we've been in the car for so long, why don't we walk a little?" Blades asked. "If we see a place that looks good, we can stop and eat."

"Are you sure?" I asked.

"Yeah. Let's get a feel for this area at least. I already memorized the street names for the one we're on, as well as the cross streets at either end of the block. Should make it easier to get back here without getting lost."

"And if we do, you can use the map on your phone again," I said.

"Who needs to ask for directions when you have something that handy? I have to say, I do like some of the new technology. Although, the thought of the damn thing listening to my every word and tracking my location isn't very comforting. I talked to one person about fishing the other day for all of two minutes, and now I keep getting ads for fishing gear. It's fucking ridiculous," he said.

I couldn't say I really understood it all either. The only technology I'd used since being kidnapped had been a TV or radio, and even then it wasn't very often.

They'd preferred us to not know what was happening in the world around us. Looking back, I wondered if they'd thought it would make us easier to manage. Or perhaps, they'd worried some of those girls would be reported as missing, and then they'd know people were searching for them and wanted them to return home.

"Wait." I reached up to touch my cheek. I hadn't learned how to cover my scars as well as Meiling did.

"You're beautiful, China. And if anyone says shit about your scars, I'll teach them a lesson they'll never forget."

I nodded and took Blades' hand, and we left the apartment and went to explore. I knew I couldn't hide forever. The fact he found me beautiful was enough. I needed to stop caring what other people might think of me.

Even though it wasn't considered tourist season, the streets were still rather busy. I clung to Blades, worried we might get separated. We peered into shop windows and checked out menus at a few restaurants before we decided on a place. Since it was our first night in New Orleans, we'd decided to try some Cajun food.

Our server came over to take our order, but I hadn't quite decided on what I wanted to try. "Can you tell me what's in the gumbo?"

Someone at a nearby table snickered. "*Chère*, this is New Orleans. You don't ask what's in the gumbo."

Um. I didn't quite understand what they meant. I stared up at the server expectantly, but they merely arched their eyebrows. "So, you really can't tell me?"

"China, order the cup, then get something else as well. Then if the gumbo isn't to your taste, you still have food for dinner," Blades said. "As for me, I'll take the jambalaya, and I'd like some fried gator on the side."

It looked like he was going all out for this experience. If he could be brave and try new things, then so could I. "Then I'll have the red beans with rice and a side of gumbo."

The server noted our choices and bustled off. I only hoped we wouldn't be fighting for the only bathroom in the apartment when we called it a night. Blades reached across the table and took my hand. The soft smile on his face made it feel like I had butterflies in my stomach.

"Want to explore a little more after we eat? Or head back?" he asked.

"I think I'm ready to relax for the rest of the night. We have an entire week to play tourist."

"Sounds good." He leaned in closer and lowered his voice. "But I wasn't planning to let you rest much."

My cheeks warmed and I was suddenly eager to eat and go back to the apartment. He'd been affectionate since my first night back in his life. It wasn't like we didn't have sex on a regular basis. Even still, every time felt special and reminded me that anything could happen tomorrow. What if tonight was our last night together? I didn't want to have any more regrets. I already had enough for a lifetime.

"I love you, Robert."

"Love you too. Always have and always will. You've been mine since the first day we met, and nothing will ever change that."

"Are the two of you married?" I looked over at the older woman who'd spoken to us. "You seem like such a lovely couple, but I noticed you weren't wearing rings. Of course, these days that doesn't mean anything."

"No," Blades said. "I've been waiting nearly twenty years for her to be ready to legally be mine."

"Well, if the two of you ever decide to take that step, I'd love to design your rings." She pulled out a business card and handed it to Blades. *Marie Clare Beauregard.* "Been a designer for over fifty years. Too old now to actually make them, but my granddaughter has taken over that aspect of the business. Wedding rings are our specialty."

"We appreciate it," Blades said, pocketing the card. "I hope I can eventually wear her down."

He really wanted to marry me? I'd known he wanted me to be his and wear the property cut, but it never occurred to me he wanted an official wedding. He kept surprising me. I'd thought he'd just do that biker thing and make me his old lady. When we'd been together before, we'd never discussed marriage. He was too busy trying to keep me and our daughter hidden from the Devil's Fury. It seemed the club wasn't the only thing that had changed over the years.

"I know that look," he said. "We can discuss it more later."

"Here's your dinner," the server said, placing our dishes in front of us, and a basket of sliced bread in the center of the table. She topped off our drinks, made sure we didn't need anything else, then hurried off to check on her other customers.

I hesitantly took a small bite of the gumbo. The spices and flavors burst on my tongue, and I eagerly ate more.

"I'd slow down, *chère*," someone said.

I didn't know why until a minute later. It felt like I was sweating profusely, I knew my face had to be red, and my mouth felt like someone had set a fire inside it. I gulped down my drink, but it only seemed to make it worse.

"Eat the bread," the other customer said. "You never drink to cut spice in Cajun food."

Our server came to refill my glass as I took a huge bite of the bread. I'd eaten an entire piece and was partway through another before the burning sensation died down. I stared at the gumbo and decided it was probably better to not finish it. Instead, I worked on the red beans and rice. When the same thing happened, the jewelry designer laughed softly.

"Everything in this place is going to be too spicy for you. Eat more bread. But this time, have some every one or two bites," she said. I did as she said and managed to eat at least half my food. Blades cleaned his plate and didn't seem the least bit bothered.

He paid for our meals, left a tip, and then we walked back to the apartment. After he locked the doors, he made sure the curtains covered them, and immediately began to strip off his clothes.

"I'm going to take a shower, and I'm sure you want one too." I decided to see if we'd both fit in there together. From what I saw of the bathroom earlier, it was a normal-size tub with a handheld showerhead someone had mounted to the wall with a plastic hook.

Blades started the water and when the temperature felt right, he got in and held his hand out to me. He helped me over the side of the rub, then yanked the curtain closed. As much as I'd have liked to play in here, there wasn't enough space for something like that. Instead, we quickly washed each other and got out. He toweled us both dry.

Neither of us bothered with clothes before we made our way over to the bed. Blades kissed me long and deep, his arms wrapping around me and holding me tight against his body. He toppled us to the bed, his weight pressing me down into the soft mattress. Blades rolled, pulling me on top of him. I sat up, straddling his waist.

"Ride me, China. Show me how much you want me," he said, his voice deep and husky.

I lifted up, reaching down to wrap my fingers around his cock. I held him still as I slowly sank down onto him, taking him all the way inside me. He groaned, his gaze locked onto mine. I could see the struggle as he fought to keep control of himself. I lifted and lowered again. Riding him, slowly at first, then faster, I could feel him trembling beneath me. Pleasure built inside me, and I threw my head back, grinding against him.

It must have been too much for Blades. He gripped my hips and surged upward into me, holding me still as he took what he wanted. I came so hard I nearly screamed. Knowing we had neighbors on either side, I bit my lip to keep as quiet as possible. Blades lifted me off his cock and tossed me onto my belly. He was on his knees behind me before I even had a second to process what he was doing, then he tugged my ass up in the air and thrust into me.

I gripped the covers and buried my face against the bed, muffling my cries as he pounded into me. My hand shook as I reached between my legs and rubbed my clit. Fast, tight circles had me so close to coming again. He shifted the angle on the next stroke as he buried himself inside me, and it was just enough to trigger another orgasm. I came so hard I could hear the wet noises as he fucked me. It was hard, deep, and wild.

His cock jerked inside me once. Twice. Then I felt the heat of his release. He didn't stop, continuing to thrust into me several more times. Surging into me that final time, he stopped once he was as deep as he could go. The hold he had on me was sure to leave a few bruises, but I didn't care. They were the good kind. He panted for breath, and I wanted to ask what had come over him. It hadn't been like this since we'd found each other again. Although, he'd lost control several times when we'd been younger. Of course, he'd also gone all night most of the time.

Blades pulled out and I felt our mingled release gush out and slide down my thighs. He lifted me into his arms and carried me back to the shower, where we washed for a second time. This time when we went to bed, he pulled me in close and drew the covers over us. I enjoyed cuddling with him like this.

"You know, I can see the merit of having a small place away from the compound. Maybe something in Florida or up in the mountains. Far enough away it could be considered a vacation and not easily accessible to our family and friends, yet close enough we could go whenever we wanted," he said.

"Are you just trying to find ways for us to have sex without someone knocking on the door or calling to see if they can come over?" I asked.

"You caught me. Seriously, though. I know you want to donate half the money Outlaw tucked away for you. What if we took about ten grand of what's left for a deposit on a small getaway somewhere?"

"I'd be all right with that. Or find something we could buy outright. I agree this is nice. Plus I know I won't run into anyone who knew me while I worked at the Silk Purse."

"Then we'll look into it when we get home. Figure out if you want to go to the beach when we run away from everyone, the mountains, or maybe we could find a lake cabin." He kissed the top of my head.

"Whatever you want. I don't care what it looks like as long as we can be there together."

"All right. But if we're going to be grandparents soon, maybe we should get something with at least two bedrooms. We might want to take a family vacation at some point, and it would save on getting a hotel."

"Get some sleep, my beautiful China. Tomorrow we'll go do some more sightseeing. Anything in particular you'd like to do?" he asked.

"I want to see Jackson Square, the Nature Institute, maybe go on one of the dinner cruises the apartment owners mentioned in their packet. There's a lot of other things, but those are the main ones, I think."

"Then we'll see what we can cram into tomorrow and go from there." His lips brushed mine softly. "Go to sleep. Sounds like we're going to have a busy day, and I want you to have enough energy for us to have another night like this one."

I smiled and cuddled closer to him. I'd thought my life was over all those years ago, first when he'd been sent to prison and later when I'd been kidnapped. The road for us to get back to one another had been rough for both of us, but we'd made it. We had the kind of love that never died and only became stronger even when we were apart. I knew I was one of the luckiest women in the world.

"I love you," I whispered as he softly snored next to me. It didn't matter if he heard me or not. I'd spend the rest of my life showing him what he meant to me.

Epilogue

Blades

Tonight was supposed to be our last night in New Orleans. I hadn't told China yet that we were extending our stay another two days, and we wouldn't be alone. Although, we were changing locations. Meiling and Dingo were going to be with us tonight on our dinner cruise. I'd booked our tickets for Steamboat Natchez. And since our daughter and son-in-law were in town, we were moving to a hotel near the Riverwalk. After dinner, we'd pick up our things at the apartment and meet the kids at the hotel.

I'd also placed a call to the ring designer we'd met our first night in town. Which was why I was trying to sneak out of the apartment right now. I'd waited until China was in the shower on purpose.

"China, I need to run out for just a minute," I called out. Before she could try to stop me, I left the apartment and went to the woman's shop a few streets over.

I had a feeling my woman was going to be really surprised tonight, for more than one reason. I only hoped it was the good kind and this didn't backfire on me. We'd spoken a few times during the trip about our future and what it might look like. I knew she loved me every bit as much as I loved her. Getting married seemed like the next logical step. Hell, it was more than a decade overdue.

I found the storefront and went inside. The woman we'd met at the restaurant smiled at me warmly, and I noticed a younger woman behind her, probably closer to China's age than mine.

"And so we meet again," the older woman said. "I happened to have something you might want for tonight, and I can craft a wedding band design around it. I don't have anything finalized, but I have a few sketches you can look over."

She pulled out a velvet box, then placed a sketch pad next to it on the glass case. I opened the jewelry box and let out a whistle. "Damn, that's gorgeous."

"I'm glad you approve. The ruby is a princess cut and it's a little over two carats. The band was handcrafted by my granddaughter, but the design is mine. I've already taken pictures of the ring from every angle so I won't miss any details when designing the wedding bands," she said.

"May I look at the designs?"

She opened the sketch pad, and I had to admit the woman had an insane amount of talent. She called these unfinished? They were incredible.

"As you can see, where the designs on the engagement ring band end will mark the beginning on the wedding band where they'll connect. In fact, you can either return here after your wedding or ship the rings to me and we'll be happy to permanently attach them. Otherwise, the rings will twist as she wears them and the design will be off."

"I'm sure I can convince China to come back to New Orleans without much fuss. How much is the engagement ring?" I asked.

She pursed her lips and eyed the ring before meeting my gaze. "For anyone else, I'd have asked at least three thousand because of the time that went into crafting it. However, I like you and your soon-to-be wife. Hearing some of your story, I'm inclined to give you a discount. How does twenty-five hundred sound?"

"Done. And the wedding bands?"

"I'm assuming you'd prefer less detail on yours,

maybe a more masculine counterpart to the feminine design on your wife-to-be's ring?" I nodded, that sounded pretty good. "I'll give you both for eighteen hundred. I do ask for a deposit before we actually start to craft the rings, but you can pay the balance when they're completed."

"Do you accept debit cards?" I asked.

The granddaughter came forward. "We do."

"Then I'll pay for the engagement ring today, and can I put down five hundred toward the bands? Or do you need more?"

"That will be fine," the woman said.

I paid and pocketed the engagement ring. I'd already showered so I just needed to put on some dressier clothes for the dinner. China and I had bought a few things since we'd been here. There was a pair of black pants and a gray shirt back at the apartment, with a nice belt and dress boots. My beautiful woman would be wearing a red and black cheongsam-style dress. I couldn't wait to see it on her.

Before I returned to the apartment, I bought a bouquet of flowers. If I returned empty-handed, then China would wonder where I'd been. I handed them to her when I entered the apartment and kissed her cheek. She took my breath away with how gorgeous she was, especially in her new dress and shoes.

"You're stunning," I said.

Her cheeks flushed and she gave me a bashful smile. "You're too sweet, Robert. Hurry and change. You said we had to be at the dock by a certain time. If we're late, we'll miss our dinner cruise."

I stripped out of my clothes and put on the new ones. Except I needed to transfer the ring from my jeans to the dress pants. China didn't seem too eager to leave my sight.

"Will you see if my cologne is in the bathroom?" I asked. "I think I left it in there."

She turned and walked off, giving me the perfect opportunity to move the ring to the pants I was currently wearing. I finished dressing, took the cologne from her, and spritzed some. Just enough to smell nice, but not so much they'd know I was coming from a mile away.

"Ready?" I asked.

She nodded and held out her hand. I wasn't about to make her walk all the way there. Instead, we went to the parking area for the apartments and got into our SUV. I drove to our destination and made sure to lock the car when we got out. Meiling and Dingo were supposed to be on board before us. They'd made sure to get here early enough to be toward the head of the line. With China and I at the tail end, I knew it wasn't likely she'd spot them.

It didn't take long for everyone to board and the steamboat to pull away from the dock. I spotted Dingo heading our way and couldn't wait to see China's face.

"Hi, Mom," Meiling said.

China gasped and turned to face her. "Meiling? Dingo? What are the two of you doing here?"

"Surprise," I said. "I invited them to have dinner with us tonight, and we'll be moving to a hotel near the Riverwalk so we can extend our stay two more days. I thought you might like going to the last few places we missed and sharing those memories with our daughter and son-in-law."

"Oh, Robert!" China reached up to lightly touch my cheek. "This is perfect. Thank you."

I felt the weight of the ring in my pocket and knew it was now or never. Dropping to one knee, which was a lot damn harder than it used to be, I held up the box for her to see.

"China. Xi-wang. The woman who's held my heart all these years, given me a beautiful daughter, and continues to brighten my days. I know I'm going to love you until the day I die. Will you do me the honor of marrying me?"

Her jaw dropped and she stared at the ring, then at me. This wasn't quite the way I'd seen this going. When she didn't answer, I started to worry I'd fucked things up. I cleared my throat and stood, snapping the ring box closed.

"Mom, what's wrong?" Meiling asked.

"Nothing, I just..." She stared at the box in my hand, then at me again. "If I say yes, will you give me as much time as I need to be ready for the actual wedding? Even if it's years from now?"

"Don't feel pressured," I said. "Maybe this wasn't the best idea."

She moved closer and placed her hand on my chest. "Robert, I love you more than anything, and I know I never want to leave your side. But I'm still healing from what happened to me, and there are times I still don't feel worthy of you. I want to say yes. There's nothing I would love more than to wear your ring and share your last name. I just need to know if I say yes now what your expectations will be."

"We can move at whatever pace you want," I said. "Even if that means we never walk down the aisle."

"Then yes, I'd love to marry you -- someday."

I opened the box and slid the ring onto her finger. I'd still buy the wedding bands, but I'd tuck them away until she was ready. And I hadn't lied. I'd wait as long as it took, even if she was never ready. All that mattered to me was having her in my life. The ring was a perfect fit and looked as if it had been made for her. She went up on her tiptoes and I leaned down to meet her halfway. Her lips brushed mine, and I saw a flash go off.

"Sorry," Dingo said. "Thought the two of you might want to have a way to remember this night forever."

"It was sweet of you to do that," China said. "Now, I believe it's time for everyone to find their tables for our meal. This has already been a wonderful night. I can't imagine it getting any better."

"Sounds like a challenge to me," I said, smiling down at her. "Come on, my beautiful China."

We spent the rest of the cruise enjoying our meal and conversation with the kids. A few kind strangers even offered to take pictures of the four of us. As I watched my family, a warmth filled me. All those years in prison, I never could have imagined my life would turn out like this. Even when I'd been younger and free, I'd thought this kind of life was out of my reach. It just went to show that fate would always find a way if things were meant to be.

Whatever the future had in store for us, I knew I'd treasure every memory. From meeting our daughter to getting out of prison and reuniting with China, each step had put me on a path to something incredible. I had what I'd always wanted… a life with my family and no fear of the club destroying them. I honestly couldn't ask for anything more. This was about as perfect as it could get.

Harley Wylde

Harley Wylde is an accomplished author known for her captivating MC Romances. With an unwavering commitment to sensual storytelling, Wylde immerses her readers in an exciting world of fierce men and irresistible women. Her works exude passion, danger, and gritty realism, while still managing to end on a satisfying note each time.

When not crafting her tales, Wylde spends her time brainstorming new plotlines, indulging in a hot cup of Starbucks, or delving into a good book. She has a particular affinity for supernatural horror literature and movies. Visit Wylde's website to learn more about her works and upcoming events, and don't forget to sign up for her newsletter to receive exclusive discounts and other exciting perks.

Harley at Changeling: changelingpress.com/harley-wylde-a-196

Bad Boys Multiverse

A Bad Boy Romance
Dixie Reapers MC
Devil's Boneyard MC
Hades Abyss MC
Devil's Fury MC
Bryson Corners
Owned by the Mob
Reckless Kings MC
Devoted Guardians MC
Savage Raptors MC
Underland MC
Devil's Boneyard MC Audio
Dixie Reapers MC Print
Dixie Reapers MC Audio
Hades Abyss MC Audio

Changeling Press LLC

Contemporary Action Adventure, Sci-Fi, Steampunk, Dark Fantasy, Urban Fantasy, Paranormal, and BDSM Romance available in e-book, audio, and print format at ChangelingPress.com – MC Romance, Werewolves, Vampires, Dragons, Shapeshifters and Horror -- Tales from the edge of your imagination.

Where can I get Changeling Press Books?

Changeling Press e-books are available at ChangelingPress.com, Amazon, Apple Books, Barnes & Noble, Kobo, Smashwords, and other online retailers, including Everand Subscription and Kobo Subscription Services. Print books are available at Amazon, Barnes and Noble, and by ISBN special order through your local bookstores.

Changeling Press, LLC

ChangelingPress.com

www.ingramcontent.com/pod-product-compliance
Lightning Source LLC
Chambersburg PA
CBHW060546260626
47161CB00003B/1076